"Why do you want to marry *me*, Guy?"

Guy smiled faintly as he returned Lucie's stony glare. "Because I fell in love with you that night in Paris three years ago, and I've been in love ever since?"

"I don't believe you," Lucie said icily.

"Well, more objectively speaking, as bank chairman I'm in need of a beautiful, poised wife." Guy's eyes traveled over her slowly. "You, Lucie Martin, seem to fit the bill."

"Why choose someone who dislikes you as much as I do?" Lucie threw back.

"A little dislike can be very alluring." He smiled hatefully, his eyes passing downward again. "And I think we'd be very good together. You might even fall in love with me, in time."

"Never! You represent everything I detest. Is that plain enough? Do you still want to marry me?"

"Yes," he said firmly.

Marjorie Lewty is a born romantic. "It's all in the way you look at the world," she suggests. "Maybe if I hadn't been lucky enough to find love myself—in my parents, my husband, my children—I might have viewed the world with cynicism." As it is, she writes about "what is surely the most important and exciting part of growing up . . . and that is falling in love." She and her family live in Leamington, a pleasant town full of beautiful parks and old Georgian homes.

Books by Marjorie Lewty

HARLEQUIN ROMANCE
2331—A CERTAIN SMILE
2382—PRISONER IN PARADISE
2421—LOVE IS A DANGEROUS GAME
2450—BEYOND THE LAGOON
2498—A GIRL BEWITCHED
2546—MAKESHIFT MARRIAGE
2579—ONE WHO KISSES
2587—DANGEROUS MALE
2650—RIVIERA ROMANCE
2678—LOVERS' KNOT
2746—A LAKE IN KYOTO
2848—IN LOVE WITH THE MAN

HARLEQUIN PRESENTS
140—THE FIRE IN THE DIAMOND
875—ACAPULCO MOONLIGHT
932—VILLA IN THE SUN

Honeymoon Island

Marjorie Lewty

Harlequin Books

TORONTO • NEW YORK • LONDON
AMSTERDAM • PARIS • SYDNEY • HAMBURG
STOCKHOLM • ATHENS • TOKYO • MILAN

Original hardcover edition published in 1987
by Mills & Boon Limited

ISBN 0-373-17006-8

Harlequin Romance first edition January 1988

My sincere and grateful thanks to Mr. Cliff
Miller,
glass sculptor par excellence,
who gave so generously of his time and expertise.

CHAPTER ONE

SHE ran up the stairs to her bedsitter on the top floor, stamping the snow from her black suede boots on to the worn lino, humming the latest pop tune as she went. A tallish girl, dark and rather beautiful, her raincoat belted in tightly round her slim waist, and a smile on her lips that seemed to announce to the world in general that it was a lovely day.

The homegoing crowd trudging along the London street outside might well have questioned that. Actually it was a pig of a day. It had been snowing and sleeting on and off all day, and the London pavements were thick with slush that was now beginning to freeze. And, just to make things worse, a fog was coming down to accompany the dusk.

But nothing could have dampened Lucie Martin's spirits just then. She had just come from a publisher's party to launch her very first children's book and under her arm she carried a parcel containing six complimentary copies. She couldn't wait to unpack it and gloat over them again.

And to make everything specially nice, Peter Philips, who worked for her publisher and had been at the party, was following her home as soon as he could get away and they were going out for a celebration meal—Chinese style. What more, Lucie

asked herself, putting her key in the lock, could any
girl ask of life?

Surprisingly, the door was on the latch. Her
stomach jolted. Who? What? Burglars? Lucie
hesitated only a second and then drew in a quick
breath and threw open the door. Light poured out to
meet her. The gas fire had been lit and before it, in a
chair that looked much too small for him, sprawled a
very large man in a dark-coloured business suit.

'James!' squeaked Lucie. She dropped her parcel
and tossed back her shining mane of silky dark hair
as she propelled herself across the room. 'Oh, James
darling, how lovely to see you! It's been ages—all of a
month. This has made my day absolutely perfect!'

Her half-brother enclosed her slim form in a bear-
hug. 'Great to see you too, Sis. The good lady on the
ground floor let me in.' He held her away and looked
down into her small, radiant face. 'You're looking
blooming. How's things?'

'Things,' she said, 'are absolutely super.' She
picked up the parcel and tore off the wrapping to
disclose a neat double pile of slim books. 'Published
today. Look!' She brandished one of the books
before her brother's eyes. 'Caterpillars at Home.
Written and illustrated by Lucie Martin.'

James took the book and flicked through the
glossy pages with their small, exquisite coloured
drawings of many different varieties of caterpillar.
'Splendid, Sis, congratulations. You've done marvel-
lously—all your dreams coming true. May I take one
home for the girls?'

'Of course. One for each of them—duly autographed.' Suddenly Lucie became serious. 'Oh, James, you can't think what this means to me. Not just the excitement of having a book published, but it's sort of justified what I did three years ago when I walked out on Father and my old life of luxury.' She smiled at the extravagant term. 'I'm my own person now, independent, free to make my own decisions and choose my own way of life. And I can pay you back the money you lent me when I turned up on your doorstep that day. It seems a whole lifetime ago.'

'I don't want——' James began, but Lucie stopped him.

'You *must* let me pay it back, I insist. I can do it out of the advance on royalties and still have quite a bit over. They've accepted my second book—that's the hedgehog one—and I've packed in my job at the café to begin work on my next opus. My darling publishers have offered to pay me a small retainer while I work at it. I've got lots of ideas. I think it's going to be about tropical fish, they're such lovely colours. But enough about me.'

She threw her raincoat over the back of a chair and smoothed her amber jersey dress over her hips with care. It was one of the items of clothing she had brought with her when she finally packed her bag at the house in Paris. She had lost weight, but it looked almost as good as new. One of the few useful things she had learned at her finishing school in Switzerland was how to wear clothes with flair. 'I want to hear all about you—and Angela, and my god-daughters. I haven't heard your news for ages. Can you stay for a meal? Peter Philips is coming round and we're going to eat Chinese, but I'd love it if you'd join us. You remember Peter—you met him last time you were here.'

James regarded his young half-sister, fair thick brows raised over quizzical hazel eyes. 'Serious?'

'Peter? Oh no, just good friends, as they say. We're both hooked on books and talk shop all the time. Peter wants to start his own agency, but it's the old, old story—no money. Can you stay?' she asked James again.

'Sorry, I'd love to, Sis, but this is only a flying visit. I've got to get across to Euston for the next Birmingham train. It makes things—difficult—if I'm late.' A frown creased his wide brow. 'Angela gets—worried.'

Lucie crossed the room to the little curtained-off kitchenette and switched on the kettle. 'Well, at least you can have a quick cup of coffee before you go out into the cold, cold snow.'

Spooning instant coffee into two mugs, she thought that 'worried' was not quite the right word to apply to Angela. Pretty, spoilt Angela who had no idea of what it meant to run a company like James's. Who whined and pouted when he wasn't always available to take her out and fall in with her whims. And now the twins were at a weekly boarding school, and with a daily help and a lovely labour-saving house in Solihull, Angela would have far too much time on her hands.

When she carried the coffee-mugs back to the fireside James was inspecting her book, turning over the pages with an approving smile. 'This is really good, Sis. The drawings of the caterpillars among the leaves and flowers are quite superb. You're a very gifted young woman—do you think you inherited it from your mother?'

Lucie nodded, her face suddenly sad. 'I like to think so. I'm sure she would have got somewhere with her art—if she had lived. And if Father had been even half-way sympathetic about it,' she added bitterly. Lucie's mother had been Warren Martin's second wife. His first marriage, to James's mother, had ended in divorce. He was now well into his third—to a film starlet. Which had been one—but only one—of the reasons for Lucie leaving home three years ago, after a blazing row the memory of which still made her feel weak at the knees.

James cupped his big hands round his coffee-mug, looking into the fire. 'Sympathy is not exactly one of our revered father's strong lines.'

'Too true,' murmured Lucie. 'Perhaps it's the only luxury that millionaire tycoons *can't* afford. Which,' she added with a small grin, 'is why I avoid millionaire tycoons. Not that I encounter many these days.'

James laughed, but she thought she heard an uneasy note in his laughter. She knew her brother so well and could always tell when he was bothered about something.

'What's up, Jimmy?' She reached over and touched his arm. 'Something's happened, hasn't it?' Her first thought was of Angela. She had a horrid feeling that James's marriage wasn't any too secure these days.

But James was evidently not thinking of his own worries. He reached into his pocket and drew out a sealed envelope. 'This came today, enclosed in a letter to me. I've no idea what's in it, of course, but I thought you should have it straight away—which is why I came along here after my business meeting in the City, to give it to you personally.' He added with his endearingly shy smile, 'I thought you might be glad of a bit of support while you read it.'

Lucie took the envelope and stared down at the words written in a flamboyant black handwriting that was all too familiar. 'Miss Lucie Martin, c/o James Martin. Please forward.'

She put down her coffee-mug and met her brother's watchful eyes, the colour draining from her face. 'From Father?'

'I'm afraid so,' James said wryly.

Painfully, Lucie's mind slipped back more than three years, since she had parted so hurtfully from her father. She could still see his handsome face contorted with rage, hear his furious voice shouting, 'All right then, get out and stay out, you little bitch, if that's what you want, but don't come grovelling back to me when you're broke!'

It hadn't been easy, coping, and without James's help she wouldn't have made it to where she was now. Certainly she wouldn't have grovelled—not to her father or anyone else—and after all the things she had said to him three years ago she hadn't expected to hear from him again. Why now, then? She ripped open the envelope with shaking fingers.

'My dear Lucie,' her father had written, 'I am sending this to you via James as I have no idea where you are. Now and then James mentions that you are well, but I'm afraid that is all I know of you.

'I can hardly believe it myself, but I'll be sixty-five in ten days, and the time has come to forget old grievances. Perhaps I was wrong, if so, be generous and give me a chance to say I'm sorry. I'm giving a small birthday party at the apartment here next week and I should dearly like my only daughter to be there. Hop on a plane and join me. If you're not too proud to accept, I enclose a banker's draft to cover the first-class return fare via Miami. It has to be a return— they won't let you in on a single, in case you fall for this idyllic spot and decide to stay and bring all your relations! This is a superb place, and the best time of the year—sun and sand and sea—well worth exchanging England for in January for a few days. Do come, it would mean a good deal to me. Your loving (please believe me) Father.

'P.S. Don't worry about meeting Stephanie. She won't be here.'

Her eyes went to the address at the top of the page: Villa Casuarina, Seven Mile Beach, Grand Cayman, British West Indies.

She handed the letter to James without a word. He skimmed through it, frowning, while Lucie picked up her coffee-mug and wrapped her cold fingers round it. She felt confused and shaken to her very depths. Why did this have to happen, to churn up her

life again when things were going along so smoothly
and happily?

James put down the letter. 'Well!' That seemed to
be all he could think of to say.

Lucie said, 'Did you know he was there—in the
Cayman Islands? I thought you said he was in South
America somewhere.'

James nodded. 'He was. He moved to the
Caymans four or five months ago. Most of his
companies—including mine—are registered there,
it's convenient for lots of reasons.' James managed
one of his father's smaller companies, situated in the
Midlands, which manufactured food containers.
'I've been trying to persuade him to put more capital
into the business so that we can expand and go after
exports more actively, but I can't get any firm
commitment from him. I expect he's up to his eyes in
some new take-over deal. You know what he's like.'

'Yes,' said Lucie, 'I know.'

There was a silence, then James said tentatively,
'Will you go, do you think?'

'To a lush party on a millionaire's paradise island?
Frankly, it's the last thing in the world I'd choose to
do, just when I'm dying to start work on my next
book. But—well—he *is* my father and it must have
cost him a good deal to write what amounts to an
apology.' She sighed. 'And I suppose part of it was
my fault, a quarrel always has two sides to it.'

She bit the end of her little finger thoughtfully for a
moment or two and then said impulsively, 'OK then,
James, I'll come with you.'

Her brother shook his head. 'I'm not invited, Lucie.'

'Not——' Lucie's brown eyes widened and her mouth fell open. 'Not invited? He wants his only daughter at his rotten party and he hasn't got the decency to invite his only son? Right then, he can jolly well do without said daughter!' Her lips pressed themselves together firmly.

James's tolerant smile said that he was used to his young sister's quick temper where her loyalty to himself was concerned. 'Hold your horses, love! It's not quite like that. He knows very well that I couldn't take time off just now—I've got an important deal coming along which is pretty vital for the company, and of course he's informed about that. Anyway, I'll be out of circulation for a while. I'm off behind the Iron Curtain tomorrow. There may be some new markets opening up there.'

'Oh,' said Lucie, and thought for a moment. 'OK, I take it back, then.'

James waited, watching her face. 'Would you mind travelling on your own? You've kept your passport up to date, haven't you? Would you be nervous?'

'Oh Lord, no, I'm used to it. Jet-baby, that was me in the bad old days.' Backwards and forwards from school to whatever part of the world Warren Martin's vast business empire took him at any given time when her holidays came along. He had her holidays planned down to the last detail. He chose her companions and her clothes and her activities. 'Now Mother's not here you like to have some weak

female to boss around,' was one of the things she had
flung at him on that last ghastly occasion. 'Well, I'm
not going to be bossed around any longer, and I've
certainly no intention of living the sort of life Mother
had to lead. Or of marrying some financial wizard
you've set your sights on for me!'

Her memory of that final quarrel was still
devastatingly clear in her mind. She could see her
father's face, crimson with rage, his fists thumping
the table. She could see, too, the dark arrogant face
of the man he had wanted her to marry.

Guy Devereux, son of an important merchant
banker—the last man on earth she would marry.
Guy Devereux. What a stupidly pretentious name!
Just to think of him sent a shiver down her back as
she remembered his mocking, sardonic face, his
dark blue eyes glinting under winged brows—
watching her. As she remembered what had happened that night after dinner, in the rose-garden of
the Paris château——

'I'm afraid I must be off now, love.' James's voice
broke in on her disturbing memories. He was on his
feet, fumbling with the sleeves of his thick overcoat.
Lucie jumped up and helped him on with it. 'Let us
know what you decide—about going out to Father.
Ring Angela and tell her your plans. I shan't be
available for a bit.'

'I'll have to think about it,' she said. 'I'm really not
terribly keen to go.'

She scribbled loving mesages in two of her
books—one for Penny and one for Prue—and James
tucked them in his overcoat pocket and gave it a pat.

'Something to read on the plane tomorrow,' he grinned.

'For the five-to-seven-year-olds? Watch it, or you'll be led away by men in white coats!'

He was serious suddenly, his face curiously drawn. 'Truer than you think, my dear. Life has its problems.'

James was on his way to the door and he wasn't going to enlarge on that, so it was no good asking. They hugged each other tightly and Lucie told him to have a good trip and called affectionate messages to everyone as the stairs creaked under his heavy downward tread.

She went slowly back into the sitting-room, a wry little smile on her lips. Dear James, he was such a *nice* man. All her life she had gone to him with her troubles, and he had never failed her. She wished she could help him now with whatever was bothering him, but if it were something to do with Angela he wouldn't tell her, he was much too loyal to the pretty wife he adored.

She washed up the coffee-mugs and went across to the opposite side of the room to brush her hair and renew her make-up. Peter would be here soon, and she almost wished she hadn't promised to go out with him to celebrate. It was going to be difficult to recapture her earlier mood of euphoria. She sat down in front of the gas fire and picked up the letter from her father again.

She was still frowning over it ten minutes later when she heard Peter's quick tread on the stairs outside and his rat-a-tat at the door. 'Come in, it's open,' she called.

Peter breezed in, admitting a keen draught from the landing. He was a tall, thin man in his late twenties, with smooth fair hair and wide-awake eyes. He carried a bottle under one arm and an assortment of brown paper bags in the other hand, from which escaped the unmistakable aroma of Chinese cooking.

'Hello again, Lucie darling. Here I am, complete with celebration meal. If it's OK with you I thought it'd be nicer to eat here, rather than brave the elements again. It's an absolutely foul evening. D'you mind a take-away?'

'No, of course not. Good idea.' She took the bags across to the kitchenette and put plates to warm under the grill. 'How much do I owe you?' It was agreed that she and Peter shared all expenses when they went out together.

'Came to eight-forty altogether. But I'm paying for the wine. My way of saying congrats, Lucie.'

He took off his coat and hung it up behind the door and went over to the fire, rubbing his hands and looking appreciatively round the long, low room. 'This is cosy.'

Over the years Lucie had managed to do all the usual things that make a bedsitter more like home: bright curtains and cushions, a handmade rug in front of the gas fire, pictures on the walls, her own drawings mingling with modern prints. At one end of the room a divan and a white melamine wardrobe-cum-dressing-table served as a bedroom. At the other a tiny kitchenette provided cooking facilities. The middle of the room was studio-lounge. Mostly studio; the lounge consisted of a couple of easy chairs.

It was a squash, but it had worked up to now and Lucie loved every bit of it. The important thing was that it was her own; she had made it possible by her own efforts, and she had never regretted the life of luxury with her father that she had left behind. In fact, until the letter arrived this evening she hadn't thought of her father for weeks.

But the letter had shaken her considerably. A frown had settled between her prettily-marked dark brows and when she carried the plates back to the small table in front of the fire Peter looked at her curiously. 'What's up, Lucie? You're not the carefree young celebrity you were at the party a while ago. Not bothered about me inviting myself here, are you?' He grinned his crooked, attractive grin. 'I assure you your maidenly virtue is safe with me, a promise is a promise. I have no base motive. Blame the filthy weather.'

Lucie shook her head, smiling back at him as she arranged the plastic containers, with their still-steaming-hot contents on the table. 'No, it's not that, Peter. I trust your honour as a British gentleman.'

'Thanks, pal.' He drew up chairs for them both. 'What's up, then? Tell Uncle Peter.'

Lucie nibbled a prawn cracker. Her appetite seemed to have gone, along with her euphoria, but Peter had taken trouble over his selection of Chinese specialities, and the least she could do was to

appreciate them. So she helped herself to a plateful
of chop suey, prawn, sweet and sour pork and rice
and said, 'When we've eaten, perhaps I will.'

He nodded and started to talk about her book and
expectations of sales, and the possible publication
date of the next one, and it wasn't until they had
cleared the table and pulled up the two easy chairs to
the fire with the coffee percolator on the hearth that
he said, 'Well?'

Lucie hesitated a moment, then she said, 'I've had
a letter from my father. It's thrown me, rather.'

Peter nodded sympathetically. 'Parents can be
trying.'

'My father's more than trying, I'm afraid.' She
hesitated again, then the need to discuss her
predicament took over. 'You see, I haven't had any
communication with him since I walked out on him
more than three years ago, and now he's written to
ask me to come to his sixty-fifth birthday party.'

'Just like that?'

'We-ell, he does say that he might have been to
blame for—things that went wrong. It isn't like him
to eat humble pie, I feel he must really want to see
me. I keep thinking that perhaps he's got some
illness that he's not telling people about. If he—if he
died, and I hadn't gone to see him when he tried to
make up our quarrel it would be really awful.'

'H'm. Sixty-five, you said? That's rather ancient
to be your father, surely? How old are you, Lucie?'

'Twenty-two next month. He must have been well
over forty when he married my mother. That was
after the divorce from his first wife.'

'And then another divorce?'

Lucie shook her head sadly. 'No, my mother died when I was fifteen. I loved her very much.'

The room was silent for a while with only the muffled sound of traffic from the snow-covered road outside, and the companionable hiss of the gas fire. Then Peter said, 'Well, surely it's not much of a problem? You could just put in an appearance and see how things were. Probably the old boy's just feeling his age a bit.'

Lucie smiled wryly. 'It's rather more than putting in an appearance. It means travelling quite a way.'

'Where is he, then?'

'The Cayman Islands.'

Peter's fair brows shot up. 'The Cayman Islands?'

'You know—in the Caribbean. Not so far from Jamaica.'

'Yes, I know,' he said slowly. And then, 'You never told me about your father, Lucie. I thought you were alone, except for your brother James.'

'I don't talk about my father. Our parting was distinctly traumatic. This letter—it's brought it all back.' She bit her lip hard.

'Yes, I could see there was something,' Peter said quietly.

She looked at him as he leant back comfortably in his chair. He was an attractive man—charming. An amusing, easy-going companion, understanding, sympathetic. And he had taken such an interest in her and her book from the day, nearly a year ago, when she walked into the publisher's office with her portfolio of drawings under her arm and her knees shaking with nerves.

At first they had met only in the office; then, one day, he had suggested they have a snack-bar lunch together to discuss the book's cover. After their first dinner-date he had kissed her in the taxi on the way back to her flat, and waited to be invited in.

It was then that she had had to explain to him that she had made a vow to keep romance out of her life until she managed to publish her first book. 'P'raps you'd rather call it a day?' she had suggested, and she had been really rather torn, because she liked him a lot.

She had been surprised and pleased when he said No, he'd like to go on seeing her now and again, with no strings attached, and that was how it had been. They had met fairly often and had lunch or dinner together, and talked about books and about their aims in life: hers to make a name as author and illustrator of nature books for children, his to have his own literary agency. Lucie found herself looking forward to their meetings more and more and wondering if she was, perhaps, falling in love with him. He had never made a pass at her after that first date, and she took it for granted that he had girl-friends who were more—obliging than she allowed herself to be.

Looking at him now, with the firelight throwing a soft glow on his smooth gold hair, she wondered how it would have been if she had been less dedicated to her work, and suddenly the defences that she had put up when she had chosen to leave her luxurious, protected existence and make her own way out in the world crumbled.

'Want to talk about it?' asked Peter. 'About your father?'

Lucie turned her head and looked into the fire. 'I adored him when I was little,' she said. 'He's a big man—big in every way—a flamboyant character. I had everything a girl growing up could want—clothes, parties, ponies, dancing lessons. I wanted to please him always, to look nice for him, to do what he wanted.'

'He's a businessman?' Peter prompted.

'Oh yes, very much so. You'd call him a financier, I suppose. He owns I don't know how many companies all over the place. My brother James—he's my half-brother really—manages one of them up in Birmingham. James was marvellous to me when I left home. I lived with him and his family for a while and went to part-time art classes. Then when my course came to an end I wanted to go it alone and I came to London and got various jobs, mostly in shops and cafés—and worked on my painting at nights and early in the mornings.'

'An independent young woman,' Peter smiled. 'But you haven't told me why you left home. Couldn't you have worked just as well on your art there? If your father was such an indulgent parent, I wonder you didn't.'

'Indulgent—ha! That's what I thought—until I wanted to do something that he didn't want me to do. And I wouldn't do something that he did, if you know what I mean. It all boiled up until in the end I just—walked out.'

'Go on,' he said.

She thought for a time and then said slowly, 'I think I first began to realise what he was like when my mother became ill. He was impatient with illness, he just didn't want to know. It was my long school holiday, and I sat with her a lot and she talked to me, and I began to understand how frustrated she had been. She wanted to be an artist—she was talented, I'm sure—but he wouldn't have it. He put every possible difficulty in her way. She had to be at his beck and call, always. She'd kept cheerful for my sake, but when she was ill she couldn't keep it up any longer. One of the things she said before she—she became unable to talk much was, "Just be careful not to let him run your life, Lucie darling. He'll try."'

'And he did?'

'Oh yes, indeed he did.' Lucie's soft mouth drew down. 'It really began when I left school. I wanted desperately to go on to art school, my art mistress encouraged me—said I had talent. But he wouldn't hear of it. He'd arranged—without my knowledge—to send me to a finishing school in Switzerland. I endured one term and that was enough—I came home. Finishing schools just weren't my line and I was crazy to go to art school. My father and I quarrelled about it all the time and I began to see what he was really like when he was opposed. Ruthless, dictatorial, sometimes almost savage. A man with an outsized ego whom everyone had to obey—or else——'

'So you walked out on him?'

'Oh, not right away. I tried to come to terms with the situation. Spent sleepless nights wondering how I could cope. I felt almost sorry for him sometimes because I knew that if I left he would be quite alone, and in his own way he loved me. Then he married again—a girl half his age called Stephanie, a film starlet, and we moved to Paris. I—to put it mildly, Stephanie and I didn't hit it off. I knew this was irritating my father, but the crunch came when he told me he wanted me to marry a business associate of his—the son of his banker. He actually admitted that the marriage would be a good thing for him— my father—in his business affairs. I thought he was joking at first, but he wasn't. We had a blazing row— everything that had been simmering under the surface came out. It was—it was horrible.' She put a hand over her eyes as if to shut out the memory. 'Next morning I packed a bag and left. I went to Birmingham, to my brother James.'

'And that was it?' Peter said gently.

'That was it. I'd done the unforgivable thing, as far as my father was concerned. The break was complete—until today.'

She refilled their coffee-cups. 'I don't know,' she said. 'I really don't know. What do you think I should do, Peter? Here, read his letter.' She passed over the thick sheet of paper with its impressive letter-heading.

They had turned out the overhead light and the room was lit dimly by the Anglepoise lamp on Lucie's drawing-table. Peter leaned forward to let the firelight play on the single sheet. At last he said,

'Do you really want my advice, Lucie?'

'Yes, I think I do. I might not take it, of course,'
she added with a faint smile.

He handed the letter back to her, giving her hand a
squeeze as he did so. 'Independent little cuss, aren't
you? Well, for what it's worth, my advice is that you
should go. As you said, you might feel guilty later on
if you didn't.'

She nodded slowly. 'I was afraid you'd say that,
and it's what I know in my heart I should do. It's just
that—it's been such a long time and—to go back
alone into my father's plushy life-style after this'—
she waved a hand round the modest, cosy room—
'which is really much more "me", is rather a
daunting prospect. It wouldn't be so bad if James
were coming with me, but he's got an important
business deal on and he can't possibly get away. Oh,
bother!' She put down her coffee-cup with a clatter,
letting out an exasperated sigh.

There was another long silence. Then, 'Lucie——'
Peter began.

'Um?' She looked up absently.

'I've got an idea. How would it be if I came along
with you?' He was watching her face and he went on
quickly, 'I'm afraid I couldn't run to first class, but
the money your father has sent you would almost
cover both our fares if we went economy class—we'd
have to shop around. What do you think? At least
you wouldn't be on your own going into the lion's
den.' He grinned encouragingly.

'Oh, Peter, that would be lovely! I'd love to have
you there with me, only——' she hesitated '—only

it's such a "family" sort of situation and it's going to
be rather nerve-racking, meeting him again after
what's happened and——'

'—and it wouldn't be quite on, to have a stranger
hanging around,' Peter put in. 'Yes, I can see that.'
He leaned over and took her hands in his. 'But what
if I weren't a stranger, Lucie?' he said, and his voice
was deeper and more serious than she had ever heard
it. 'What if I were the man you were going to marry?'

Her eyes widened. 'Peter—I——'

'Don't say anything, darling. I know it's a bit of a
shock. I've wanted to say this for ages, but I've been
biding my time. I could see you weren't a girl to be
rushed off her feet and I agreed to your terms.' He
smiled his crooked smile. 'There's been no other girl
since the first time I saw you in Frank Blessington's
office with the sun shining through the dusty
window, your eyes like wallflowers, and your hair all
shiny like a blackbird's wing.'

'Oh, Peter——' Lucie laughed shakily. 'Be
serious!'

'I was never more serious in my life. I thought
then, That's the girl I want—for keeps. I'm in love
with you, darling Lucie, and I want us to be married.
Say you'll think about it. Say we can go to your father
together and ask his blessing. Will you, Lucie?'

It was too much, all at once. First the letter, then
this. She couldn't manage to think straight.

Peter slipped down on to the rug at her feet, gazing
up at her. 'Oh, darling, I've waited so long,' he
groaned, and she remembered how patient and

understanding he had been. She had thought he had other girls, but all this time he had waited for her—it was somehow touching and rather humbling.

She said impulsively, 'I'd love you to come with me, if I go to the Caymans, but—but—about getting engaged—it's taken me by surprise. I can't——' she began to giggle a little hysterically. 'Oh dear, this sounds like the Victorian novels when the heroines murmured, "This is so sudden!" and promptly fainted away.'

Peter matched her mood. 'And here I am on my knees,' he grinned his lopsided grin, 'proposing according to the accepted custom of those days. Customs change, but there's one thing that doesn't— I bet the Victorian gent was just as much in love with his crinolined lady as I am with you, my darling. And I bet she wasn't half as lovely.'

Lucie nearly melted. Peter was such a dear and she liked him so much. But marriage——!

'I can't promise, Peter. I don't think I'm ready to commit myself yet to anything but my art, it means pretty well everything to me. Does that sound horribly pretentious?'

He shook his head. 'Of course it doesn't, you're a very talented girl and you're dead right to be serious about your art. I'm afraid I've rushed my fences—I meant to wait a bit longer. And then this thing about your father came up and it seemed like a good time.' He sounded so despondent that she wanted to lean down and kiss and comfort him.

But instead she said slowly, 'But it *would* be lovely if you could come with me on this trip. It would make all the difference.'

Peter raised his head eagerly. 'To me, too. Look, couldn't we work something out? We could be sort of engaged as far as the outside world is concerned, for the time we're out there. That would give you an excuse for taking me along. And when we get home we could formally decide to call it off. That is, of course,' he added, 'if the romantic sunsets in the Caribbean haven't softened your heart and made you fall desperately in love with me.'

She began to laugh. 'Peter, you're wonderful, and I think it's a splendid idea. At least we'll have a holiday and have some fun.' She stood up and pulled him to his feet beside her. 'Thank you for being such a good friend,' she said.

He pulled a face at that. 'No more?' he said softly, his hands at her waist. 'It's been a good day—the party, and your book and everything. Couldn't we end it the proper way?' He pulled her closer and she could feel his heart begin to race. He stroked her neck and his hand found its way inside her blouse and began to mould her breast gently. 'Lucie,' he groaned, and his mouth closed over hers.

Another moment and it would be too late. Another moment and her mind would stop working, her body would take over. It would be so easy to let her lips relax, to press against him, to let him lead her over to the divan.

But too much had happened today and she was off balance. She didn't want her first lovemaking to be like this—the impulse of a moment. She pushed away from him. 'Peter, you promised. I'm not—not ready——'

He let her go rather abruptly and walked over to the door to unhook his coat. 'OK, Lucie, I can wait a bit longer. But now I think I'd better go down and cool off in the snow.'

He wasn't taking offence; he really was a nice man. She went with him to the top of the stairs.

'Let's meet for lunch tomorrow at the Oak Tree and we can discuss arrangements,' she said. 'Good-night, Peter, and—and thanks.'

He bowed from the waist with exaggerated gallantry. 'Thank *you*, my lady.' At the turn in the stairs he stopped and looked back with a thumbs-up gesture. 'See ya, baby!' he shouted, and she waved to him, laughing. She went slowly back into the flat and closed the door.

She lay awake for a long time after she finally got into bed, thinking of the past—hoping that there could be a healing of wounds with her father. Remembering that last horrible quarrel.

It all got very jumbled up and finally her eyelids began to ache with tiredness. And her last thought was of Peter. I can go back and face Father now, with Peter beside me. And if he's got any more men like that hateful Guy Devereux lined up for me it'll be just too bad!

CHAPTER TWO

'THIS is what I call the life.' Peter laid back his head as the taxi drove them away from the little airport in Grand Cayman a week later, and sighed deeply and with pleasure. 'How did you ever bring yourself to cut adrift and exchange this sort of life for a bedsitter in Bayswater, darling?'

'I've explained that.' Lucie sat bolt upright, her fingers lacing themselves together. At this moment the sunshine and the limpid blue sky and the glimpses of the luxury hotels and apartment buildings between the lushly-growing trees and flowering shrubs were doing nothing at all for her spirits, which were just about at zero. Ever since she had sent the cable to her father saying tersely, 'Arriving Thursday Lucie', she had been feeling more and more depressed, and now that she was here, in this beautiful paradise island, all she really wanted to do was to go back to Bayswater and get on with her book.

Which was absurd really, she scolded herself. Peter was going to love every second of it, and why shouldn't he? He'd taken care of all the preliminary arrangements and he'd been sweet to her on the journey, apologetically trying to make it up to her for having to travel economy class, when, without him, she might have booked first class. Not that she had cared about that. Flying first class would have been more comfortable, certainly, but it wouldn't have been any novelty to her. First-class travel had been taken for granted in her old life, and on this particular trip all the first-class perks—the champagne, the free drinks, the extra leg-room, the choice of menu, the hovering and attentive stewardesses who pander so beautifully to the needs and whims of first-class passengers—would have meant nothing at all to her.

And now she was here and in a few minutes she would have to face her father. That fact loomed huge and alarming at the front of her mind, she could think of nothing else.

The taxi turned off the road into a smooth drive that wound between dense, dark-green shrubs and pulled up before one of a group of six white villas with steeply-sloping pink roofs, situated at discreet distances apart, almost on the beach.

'Trust Father to pick the best,' murmured Lucie, as Peter fished in his notecase for US dollars to pay the driver.

A smiling, dark-skinned girl came out of the villa as the taxi drove away.

'Miss Martin? I'm Blossom, your father's maid. Your father is expecting you, miss, he has just gone to the dive-shop with a friend and he will soon be back. Please let me take your bag.' She led the way into the villa.

'Service!' murmured Peter, following Lucie. He grinned and added, 'You gets what you pays for in this life.'

'Exactly,' Lucie said rather tartly. The villa seemed to represent everything that she had given up. Luxuriously furnished, with a covered balcony looking out over the sea and the white strip of sand, where a few brown bodies were stretched out on sun beds. Only a few—no tourist crowd here. A place for top people, able to pay top prices.

Peter laughed as they went into the long, cool living-room where fans whirred and deeply-cushioned chairs were placed invitingly before the sliding-glass door leading on to the verandah. 'Come on, love, it's not as bad as all that. Sit down and relax.'

Lucie met his teasing look and grinned guiltily. 'Oh, it's a perfect spot, of course it is. Lovely for a holiday. It's just that it reminds me of things I've been trying to forget, that's all.'

'Well, I can take lots of it.' Peter leaned back, half closing his eyes. 'Cat with a saucer of cream, that's me.'

She regarded him indulgently. Perhaps she was taking all this too seriously; she needed Peter here to laugh her out of it. 'You're going to be a bit of a surprise for Father, aren't you? Maybe I should have warned him. I hope there's a room for you somewhere.'

He slid her a glance. 'I suppose it wouldn't be on to share yours? No, I see it wouldn't. Daddy wouldn't approve, is that it? Ah well, I can always sleep out on the beach at a pinch, it looks distinctly inviting.'

'Don't be an idiot, Peter!' Lucie said a trifle sharply.

His face became serious and he leaned across to
cover her hand with his. 'Sorry, my sweet, just trying
to lighten the atmosphere. Nervous, are you?'

'Dithering,' she said, and indeed her teeth were
almost chattering. 'Silly, isn't it—my own father!'

His clasp tightened. 'I'm here to back you up, love.
Peter means "a rock" you know. Rock-like, that's
me.'

She gave him a grateful, fleeting smile and thought
once again how much worse it would have been if she
had been alone. But even with Peter here the
butterflies in her stomach were fluttering wildly. She
jumped up again and began to prowl round the room.
It was typical of a room in a luxury rented villa; she
had seen so many of them. Squashy lounge sofa and
chairs, low smoked-glass coffee-tables, built-in fit-
tings that housed radio, television, trailing leafy
plants. Nothing in the least home-like about it.
Magazines were piled on a side table, mostly
featuring scuba diving. A copy of the *Financial
Times*, pink and neatly folded, lay beside them. A
few brashly-coloured modern prints hung on the
walls. Not the sort of pictures that appealed to Lucie,
but she trailed round examining them, to keep her
mind occupied.

Then at the far end of the room she stopped
abruptly. Hanging in a narrow alcove was a picture
of herself, painted by her mother, when she—
Lucie—was about twelve or thirteen, all huge brown
eyes and a torrent of dark hair. Lucie hadn't seen it
for years, she had thought that her mother had
destroyed all her pictures during that ghastly time

when she had been at the end of her tether. But her
father must have found this one after her mother
died. He must have taken it with him in his
wanderings round the world. He must have cared for
her mother, in spite of the way he had treated her.

'Oh,' she gasped softly. 'He kept it—he kept it all
this time!'

Peter came and stood behind her. 'It's you, isn't it,
Lucie? You were a smasher even at that early age.'

'Thanks,' said Lucie absently, and went back to
her chair. She was trying to adjust to new and
confusing ideas.

Suddenly she stiffened as footsteps sounded
outside. He was here, her father, he was walking
along the verandah and in at the open window.
'Lucie! Lucie, my dear girl! You're really here!' A
big man, smiling uncertainly, he stopped just inside
the window.

She jumped to her feet. She had only a moment to
think, with sudden shock, 'He's changed. He's
grown *old*', and then he was holding out his arms and
she was enfolded in a giant hug and it was as if she
were a little girl again.

'Well, well, well, let's look at you.' He held her
away. 'You're just as lovely—but much too thin.
We'll have to feed you up on turtles and lobsters, and
give you a nice tan over that pale January-in-
England face.' He touched her cheek. He was
talking, she knew, to cover the awkwardness of the
meeting and set the tone of their encounter. Both of
them must have been remembering that last time,
when he stormed out of the house in Paris and she

rushed upstairs, weeping, to pack her bag.

Peter had been standing to one side and she reached for his hand. 'Father, this is Peter Philips. He came to look after me on the journey. We're going to be married.'

There was a pause and she saw the slight tightening of the muscles of her father's jaw. Then he held out a large hand. 'Glad to know you, Peter.' The two men eyed each other a trifle warily.

Lucie said, 'Sorry to spring Peter on you at the last minute, Father, but you didn't give me much time, did you, and I couldn't explain it all in a cable.' She passed over the fact that she could have phoned; a cable had saved the embarrassment of a conversation. 'Can we find Peter a room?'

Warren Martin brushed aside the difficulty. 'Oh, we'll soon fix something. Now, we must all have a drink, to celebrate your arrival.'

Lucie watched him as he walked over to a cabinet on the far side of the room. He *had* changed, there was no denying it. He wore canvas shorts and a jazzy cotton shirt open to the waist, and she could see the way the flesh had begun to sag at the back of his neck and round his knees. His hair was almost entirely white and very thin now. But he was still a handsome man, broad-faced and large-featured, and he had lost none of his old air of affluence. He was a man who had achieved, who had fought in the tough world of business and won, and every confident word and gesture proclaimed it.

'Try these, I can recommend them—speciality of the house,' he announced, handing them tall glasses containing a clear amber liquid with ice-cubes rattling in it.

Lucie gulped the drink. 'Mm, lovely—I needed that. It's just as warm as ever here. Does the sun ever stop shining in the Caymans? I suppose we're in the middle of the summer here now, only there isn't really any winter, is there?' she prattled on. Oh Lord, how corny can you get?

'Certainly not in January, my dear. Best time to come.' Warren Martin gazed at her as if he couldn't take his eyes off her face. 'God, it's great to see you again, Lucie. I've missed you like hell. By the way, Stephanie and I have split up. Six months ago. It never worked—you were right about that, dead right.' He turned to Peter. 'Forgive us, Peter? Perhaps Lucie has sketched in the family situation for you?'

He made a wry face. 'These foolish things happen—important not to let them go on too long, isn't that so, Lucie?'

'Yes,' she murmured.

Her father settled back in his chair. 'And what line are you in, Peter?' Lucie recognised that bland expression so well and knew he was summing Peter up.

Peter responded enthusiastically, and Lucie sipped her drink and watched them and listened. Her father was making a real effort to be amiable; he smiled a lot, which wasn't at all like him, and his tone was sociable, genial, as he asked questions about Peter's job, displaying interest in the publishing business, being sympathetic about Peter's plans to start his own agency. Either he was putting on a good show, Lucie thought, because he really wanted to make up their quarrel—or else he had reasons of his own to be cordial to Peter.

Oh dear, she wished she didn't know him so well. She wished she didn't have to supect his motives; but the habit of years didn't die in a few minutes and she couldn't believe that the hard, flinty edges of the man had been smoothed away.

When the talk became general he asked about her book, and it fell to Peter to enthuse about it, Lucie remaining modestly silent. Her father patted her hand and his warm congratulations seemed absolutely genuine. 'James told me about it and I want to see it—have you brought a copy for me?'

'Well I——' She hadn't. It had never occurred to her that he would ask for what could only be a proof that she had been right to pursue her ambitions and he had been wrong to try to stop her.

'I've brought one,' Peter put in eagerly, and fished in his bag for a small brown-paper parcel. 'You'll be very proud of your daughter when you see it.'

'I'm sure I shall.' Warren Martin took the parcel, smiling his unfamiliar affable smile. He's very strange, Lucie thought, I've never in my life seen him in this mood. 'Well now, you'll want to get settled in. Afraid there are only two bedrooms here, but I'll do a bit of phoning round and find a room for Peter.'

'I'm sorry to put you to so much trouble, sir.' Sir! thought Lucie, amused at Peter's air of diffident respect. But she supposed it wasn't surprising— Warren Martin had always had that effect on people.

girl. How about eating? Shall I ask Blossom to bring tea up to you?'

Lucie thanked him and said no, they seemed to have been eating snacks most of the day, and her father said, 'Right then, I'll walk along to Peter's hotel and make sure he's comfortable. I've told our guests to be here at eight, so you've plenty of time to relax.'

'What sort of a party is it? Does one dress up?'

'Dress is fairly casual here. I'm sure you'll look lovely in anything—or in nothing very much.' He grinned lovingly at her. 'We're meeting here for drinks and then we're going along to a new place called The Waves' Edge, further along the beach, for supper and dancing under the stars. Very romantic!'

'Sounds like fun,' said Lucie.

'I hope so. I'm afraid my guests won't be exactly in your age group, my dear, but at least you'll have Peter to provide the romance.' He patted her arm indulgently. 'I'll tell Blossom to wake you at seven, that'll give you time to dress. Ask her for anything you want, she's a nice girl and very willing. See you later, then.' He nodded, went across the room and closed the door softly behind him.

Lucie pulled off the well-worn suit she had travelled in and hung it up carefully. She wouldn't be wearing that again until she left for home. Here, a bikini and light cover-up was all she would need, together with beach-wear and two dresses for evening. The bikinis and sundresses she had bought at a chain-store before she left. Not exactly *Vogue*, but they were colourful and they would have to do.

But she would wear the lilac chiffon dress tonight, she decided, as she unpacked her bag and hung everything up in the clothes closet. It was her favourite and it suited her. And it wouldn't let her down in the company of her father's rich friends. It was the one dress that had an exclusive label on it— the very last thing she had bought in Paris before she left. She could have taken all her beautiful clothes with her, but that would have been absurd for the Cinderella existence that she proposed to lead. But perhaps she wouldn't be a Cinderella much longer, now that she was a published author.

She felt a little glow, thinking of her book. The excitement hadn't worn off yet. She slipped on a nylon wrap and wandered out on to the balcony. Leaning on the rail, she let her gaze take in the wide vista below—the dazzling white strip of beach, the tall palms, straight as pencils, with their heavy plumes of leaves curling over at the top, and beyond that the incredible pale green of the sea, changing to deep blue where the line of the reef crossed it. Here and there the striped colours of sails—blue and white and yellow and orange—showed like butterflies against the blue of the sea, as para-sailors skimmed over the water. Paradise island, indeed! Peter had obviously thought so. And yet—in the middle of all this beauty and glamour and luxury she felt a kind of homesickness for her cosy little flat in London, for the cheerful buzz of the gas fire and the glow of the lamp on her drawing-table. I must be mad, she thought. But she knew that if she had to choose again she would choose the same way—the only way for her.

She didn't regret it for a moment, but all the same it was a tremendous relief that her father wanted to be friends again. The break with him had left a painful wound inside her. Over the years she had walled it off until she hadn't felt the hurt any longer, but now the wall was down she examined the wound and knew that it had almost healed. He had accepted her as a person in her own right, and not someone to be dominated and ordered about. With a sigh of contentment she lay down on the soft bed and closed her eyes.

Blossom, the smiling dark-skinned maid, called her at seven and she was immediately awake. An hour to get ready—she could take her time and enjoy it. Just for once she would savour the luxury of living soft again. Humming happily under her breath, she went into the adjoining bathroom.

She was ready with three minutes to spare. She had enjoyed a perfumed soak in the aubergine bath and there had even been time to wash her hair. She put a final touch to it now, coiling it up on top of her head. Like a shiny blackbird's wing, Peter had said, extravagantly, and she smiled softly now, remembering.

He really was a darling and she liked him immensely. But love? Marriage? She thought of her mother and what marriage had done to *her* art. How obstacle after obstacle had worn down her resolve until finally she had thrown her brushes and paints and canvases into a huge box and put it out for the

rubbish collection. Lucie had come in and seen her
ripping up her paintings and had been shocked at the
look of hopelessness on her mother's lovely, sensitive
face. She had been only fourteen then, but she had
put her arms round her mother and they had wept
together and she had felt that she understood. That
was the time that she began to turn against her
father. She wished she had known, then, that he had
saved and cherished that one picture—the one of her
as a young girl, the one that was hanging in the
living-room now. He must have cared about her
mother more than he had appeared to.

Even so, he was a difficult man—an impossible
husband. There was no way she could forget that.

But how different Peter was! A rock, Peter had
called himself, and he was just that: dependable,
understanding, straightforward. And the wonderful
thing was that he liked her work and encouraged her.
She loved him for that. He understood her dedication to her art and there would never be any conflict
between them about it. They could have a sensible,
modern marriage, each one respecting the other's
needs and wishes.

And perhaps soon Peter might achieve his
ambition to have his own agency in London, that
would be really splendid. Suddenly, as she leaned
towards the mirror to stroke gold-dusted eye-shadow
over her lids, a bright idea struck her. Perhaps her
father might help Peter on the financial side. It
would be only a drop in the ocean of his vast business
enterprises and Peter would surely not be too proud
to accept a loan from his future father-in-law, just to

get him started up. Yes, that was a marvellous idea. She would have to think out how she could broach it to the two of them.

Suddenly the future looked bright. She was ready for marriage. She had so nearly let Peter make love to her on the night when her father's letter came. She looked at the big, satin-covered bed and warmth began to seep through her as she imagined herself and Peter lying there, entwined. Yes, she had denied her woman's instincts long enough.

She covered her hot cheeks with her palms. She must stop this and remember she had to meet her father's friends in a moment or two. She twirled round before the mirror and was satisfied with her choice of the lilac dress. It still fitted perfectly. The pearly skin of her neck glowed against the low, swathed neckline. The filmy skirt swished round her knees as she turned before the looking glass. She adjusted the narrow shoulder-straps, glittering with rhinestones, and wondered if her father would remember that he had paid for the dress. A smile played around her mouth. It was good, now, that she didn't mind a bit if he did remember, that she no longer felt defensive or guilty when she thought of him.

There was a tap on the door at a minute after eight and Peter came in. He had changed into silver-grey trousers with a shirt to match, and his fair hair was brushed immaculately.

'You look very smart,' Lucie smiled, as he slipped an arm round her possessively.

'And you look incredibly beautiful,' he whispered

close to her ear, planting a kiss on her shining dark hair. 'This is a super place, isn't it? My hotel is small but extremely comfortable. You must come and see my room,' he added meaningly.

'Yes.' She laughed into his eyes.

'Does that mean what I hope it means?' His arm tightened round her waist.

'Perhaps,' she teased. Soon she would tell him. 'But now we must go down and join the party.'

From the living-room came the buzz of conversation and laughter and the clink of glasses. 'Sounds like a crowd,' Lucy said, and for a moment she was sixteen again, being brought down to meet an intimidating collection of her father's business acquaintances. To be looked over and summed up. 'Pretty child—a pity she's so gauche and tongue-tied.' That was what she had heard one woman say, when she was within earshot. Lucie had seethed. Gauche, indeed! Tongue-tied! 'And you're shallow and conceited and backbiting!' she had longed to fling back. How she had hated them all! She could smile, now, for the over-critical, prejudiced child she had been.

'Not too many,' Peter was saying. 'Mostly American. Seem quite pleasant people.'

Good, thought Lucie wryly, as they entered the long living-room. Pleasant people at her father's parties would make a nice change.

Her father came across the room, glass in hand. 'Here you are, Lucie, come and meet everyone.' One arm went round her shoulder and the other waved towards his guests, disposed round the room. She was aware that he had been drinking fairly heavily already, but he had always been a man who boasted that he could hold his liquor and his voice was steady as he performed the introductions. 'Dorothy—Mary—Harriet—Steve—Frank—meet Lucie, my little girl.'

Quite the proud father, thought Lucie in amusement, responding to the chorus of 'Hi' and 'Hello' and 'Glad to meet you, Lucie'.

Peter was right, they were pleasant people—warm, friendly, family people. Very different from the guests she remembered from dinner parties in the bad old days—those hard-boiled business men and their exotic, expensive, chilly wives.

'And I'm sure you remember Guy Devereux,' her father was saying. 'Guy just dropped by a minute or two ago and I've persuaded him to join us.'

Lucie's head jerked round towards the end of the room as if it were being pulled by a string. The shock that stabbed through her was a purely physical thing, for her mind had gone numb. At the end of the room, in tight-fitting black trousers and a snowy white shirt that emphasised his darkness, a tall man was standing beside the drinks cabinet, leaning over to speak to a woman in a grey taffeta dress with a frilly collar. He lifted his head as Warren Martin spoke and Lucie met gleaming, dark-blue eyes fixed on her under lowered lids, and felt icy cold, as if she were going to faint. Guy Devereux sauntered across the room, holding out a hand. 'I hope you remember me, Lucie. I remember you very well indeed. I hear that congratulations and good wishes are in order. I hope you'll both be very happy.' The deep, mocking voice set her nerves jangling, and automatically she moved closer to Peter and put her arm through his.

'Thank you.' She couldn't meet those incredible blue eyes, instead she looked up at Peter with a trembling little smile, which could be construed as happy emotion in a young bride-to-be.

'You've just arrived, how was the weather in London?' Guy was talking to Peter now, exchanging remarks that were quite casual but watching him with that same concentrated gaze that he had fixed on her. Peter was laughing and being charming and the two men seemed to be hitting it off splendidly. Peter tried to draw her into the conversation, but her mouth was dry and all she could manage was a nod or two of agreement and a smile that was frozen on her mouth.

It was quite absurd to react like this, humiliating to discover that this man still had the power to reduce her to a zombie. She hated him, she loathed him. Finding him here was spoiling what promised to be a happy time of reunion.

As he walked away and resumed his conversation with the woman in the grey dress her knees went groggy and she sank into a chair between her father and Peter, reaching with a shaking hand for the drink that was put in front of her.

'My banker,' Warren Martin was explaining to Peter. 'One has to keep on the right side of one's banker.'

'Indeed so!' The two men exchanged a knowing smile and Lucie wanted to scream.

'Did you have to invite him, Father? You know I've always disliked the man,' she muttered in a low voice, looking up.

'Oh, Devereux's OK,' Warren Martin replied easily. 'Although he's not everyone's cup of tea, I admit.' He gave her a fond, indulgent smile and she knew he was remembering—everything. And playing down its importance to both of them.

'But he's not really your banker, is he? Surely it's his father who's the top man in the bank?'

'His father retired a few months ago. Guy holds the reins now. A big responsibility for a comparatively young man to be chairman of a private merchant bank,' he added to Peter, and Lucie saw Peter glance towards Guy with something like awe.

Chairman of his bank! That would boost the man's ego no end and make him more odiously superior than ever. 'Oh well, I'll try to bear it—only keep him away from me, that's all I ask.'

When they all drifted out to the cars that would take them to the restaurant further along Seven Mile Beach, Lucie's hopes rose as she saw Guy Devereux getting behind the wheel of a low-slung, vicious-looking convertible, and driving off in the opposite direction. 'Oh, good,' she muttered, squeezed between her father and Peter in the front seat of her father's saloon, 'the man's not joining us.'

Her father chuckled. 'He is, you know. He's just gone back to his hotel to take a phone call he's expecting from New York. He'll be along later.'

It was absurd, she told herself, as the party trailed into the restaurant, to be rocked back on her heels

like this because of a man she had met and disliked
three years ago. There was no possible way he could
pose a threat to her now. She would ignore him and
enjoy the evening.

'Nice place.' She put a hand on her father's arm as
the party settled down at tables on the vast outside
deck. Feathery palm-trees overhung the edges of the
deck, waves swished softly beneath and the lightest
of breezes stirred her hair. On each table shaded
lamps threw a golden glow over the gleaming cutlery
and glass and the posies of tiny pink and white
flowers. And above it all the dark velvet arch of the
sky was thick with stars.

'No, not merely nice,' she laughed. 'It's a fabulous
place. So clever of you to pick it!'

Her father patted her hand and smiled down at
her. He was so *glad* that they had got back to their
old, loving father-and-daughter relationship, she
could see that. It was years and years since she had
felt so close to him, not since she was in her early
teens, before her mother became ill, before she found
out the kind of man he was. But he had changed—
mellowed—she was sure of it. Oh, it was lovely to
have a father again, a father she could be proud of.
She wasn't going to allow Guy Devereux to spoil her
pleasure in their reunion.

She and her father and Peter shared a table with a
couple called Dorothy and Steven Maddox, and
when they were settled, Dorothy, a plump fiftyish
woman with thick white hair, waved to perfection,
and wearing a flowery dress, leaned towards her. 'I
hear you're an artist—do tell me about your work,

I'm sure my darling grandchildren would just love your book.'

As the meal progressed the talk flowed freely along with the wine. Lucie drank a little too much wine and laughed a great deal and kept her eyes on their own table because she wasn't sure of her reaction if she saw Guy Devereux come in to join the party.

Dorothy was a blessing in the circumstances, a non-stop narrator of her grandchildren's talents and cute sayings. Steven, her husband, was a tubby teddy-bear of a man, evidently a keen scuba diver and he and Warren Martin talked diving. Lucie remembered that her father had always enjoyed diving whenever they had lived in a part of the world where it was possible. When she was growing up he had tried to persuade her to learn to dive, but the paraphernalia of scuba diving—the clumsy backpacks and rubber wet-suits and face-masks—had never appealed to her.

The two men seemed to be making arrangements for the next day to go to Cayman Brac, one of the two 'sister' islands, and Dorothy was trying to persuade her husband against it.

'Oh, Steve, why do you want to go all that way? Flying and everything, just for a swim?'

Her husband grinned at her. 'Ah, don't call it "just a swim", girlie. Some swim! The Bob Soto diving set-up here is good but Warren here tells me that Cayman Brac is the best and I'm not finishing this vacation without diving the wall there. Why not come along with us tomorrow—flight leaves at eight-

thirty a.m. on the dot, and you're there in under an
hour. Come on, Dot, you don't need your beauty
sleep.'

His wife pulled a face at him. 'No, thank *you*. You
don't get me up at that hour!' She turned to Lucie.
'You're not going with these madmen, are you,
Lucie?'

Lucie looked at her father. 'I don't think——'

He smiled at her. 'Don't worry, love, I know you're
not interested. And anyway, you've done enough
flying for the present. You and Peter stay around
here and take it easy. We shan't be away long, shall
we, Steve? I've got an appointment at four o'clock,
anyway, so I'll have to be back by then.'

She nodded. 'OK, go and enjoy yourselves, boys.'
She would enjoy herself too, lazing away the day with
Peter under the palm trees, sipping iced drinks and
eating gorgeous seafood like the creamy concoction
that was being served up to them at this moment.

'Luvly grub!' murmured Peter. 'I could do with a
month of this kind of life. Do you know, I've never
eaten out of doors under the stars before. It's kind of
romantic.' He squeezed her thigh under the table.
'You look spectacular, darling, you're the prettiest
woman in the room.' His hand was warm and his
voice caressing.

She turned her head to smile at him, and as she did
so she encountered the dark intensely-blue gaze of
Guy Devereux, between the fronds of overhanging
palms. He must have come in some time after the
main party and he was sitting at the next table. He
was staring fixedly at her, and her stomach churned.

Peter followed her look. 'Seems I'm not the only man who thinks so,' he chuckled. 'Our macho friend from the bank has his beady eyes on you, sweet. He'd better watch it!'

There was a short silence, then Peter queried, 'What's the matter, Lucie? You look——' His eyes moved from her pale cheeks to the dark, grim face of the man at the next table and back again. 'He's not— he wouldn't be the fellow you were telling me about? The one your father tried to marry you off to when you were a teenager, would he?' When she didn't reply he nodded slowly. 'So that's the way it is. I see. He looks a fairly tough customer. Well, you needn't worry about him now, darling. He'll have me to contend with if he tries any funny business.'

He sounded quite fierce, and Lucie laughed it off with a light remark. She didn't want any awkward-ness with Guy Devereux, she just wished he wouldn't look at her.

The five-piece band on the raised platform in the corner of the deck was launching into a tune from the Top Forty, and couples were crowding on to the floor. When Peter said, 'Dance?' she stood up immediately, glad to put a distance between herself and the impact of those dark-blue, probing eyes that seemed to reach right into the very depths of her.

The small dance-floor was crowded with jiving bodies, each doing their own thing. Lucie laughed up at Peter as they jigged and dipped and twirled in the starlight. She hadn't done any disco-dancing since her art-school days, but it was something you didn't forget, like riding a bicycle—which was another

thing that belonged to her time in Birmingham with
James and Angela. She laughed up at Peter, letting
herself relax and move to the rhythm of the music.
When it finally stopped and they returned to their
table, her eyes were shining.

'That was lovely.' Lucie put her hand through
Peter's arm and squeezed it. Her cheeks were pink
and a tendril of silky black hair fell across her
forehead. She slipped into her chair next to her
father, turning half away from the next table. She
didn't even know whether Guy Devereux was still
there, and she didn't care, she assured herself.

'Enjoying yourself, poppet?' His childhood name
for her! It must be all of ten years since she had heard
it.

'Oh yes, this is a marvellous spot, I'm loving every
minute.' She took a swig from her wineglass, which
had been refilled while she was on the dance-floor.
She was a little drunk, but that was what a birthday
party was all about, and it was helping to dispel the
last vestiges of her doubts about the wisdom of
coming. Everything was turning out wonderfully
well, and tomorrow she and Peter would have a
lovely day together and she would tell him that she'd
made up her mind. She took another drink of wine.

'May I claim a dance?' Suddenly she was
conscious of a tall form standing behind her chair,
and her heart flipped. She looked towards Peter, but
he had been buttonholed by Dorothy, who was
shrieking with laughter at some story she was telling
him.

'Go and dance, poppet.' Her father gave her a

little push. 'You mustn't let Peter monopolise you. Look after her, Guy.'

'I'll do that.' The deep voice vibrated in her head. All the other sounds—the music, the laughter, the talking—faded into background noise, and only the sound of Guy Devereux's voice was real. It sounded like a threat. Lucie felt herself begin to shake inside; it was terrifying how this man affected her. But she mustn't let him know that, she mustn't let him know that she remembered that night in Paris, or that it had left any impression on her at all.

She got to her feet and let him lead her on to the floor. The band had changed to a slow, smoochy beat and couples were locked together, swaying to the music. Guy's arm went round her waist and she found her step automatically following his as they moved together. She tried to think of something to say—something light and amusing—but her mind was blank and her voice seemed to have dried up.

He was silent too, just holding her and moving slowly, almost sensuously, to the music. The very silence between them seemed to make the moment far too—too intimate. As if they had known each other for ages, as if they didn't need words to renew their acquaintance. She licked her dry lips, desperately conscious of the hard body so close against her own, her memory taking her back treacherously to that other night when he had held her, kissed her——

She swallowed hard. 'What a delightful place——' she began, but he cut off the rest of the conventional little remark.

'I came back, you know,' he said, and as she raised startled eyes, he added, 'I came back the next day, to see you, but you weren't there.'

She knew that it was no use playing a game with him—pretending not to know what he was talking about. He would see through that in a moment.

'Why?' she asked faintly.

'To apologise. To ask you to forgive me for what must have seemed unpardonable to you. I'm afraid I made the mistake of placing you with your father's somewhat sophisticated set. Your get-up suggested that you were much older than I took you for. If I'd known you were so young, so——'

'Naïve?'

'Let's say inexperienced.' she heard the faint smile in his voice.

'Well, I was—*then*.' She wriggled in his arms. 'Shall we sit down now?'

His hold tightened. 'Not yet. I've apologised—a bit late in the day, but that wasn't my fault. The least you can do, Miss Lucie Martin, is to accept my apology. I'd like us to be friends. Your father——'

'Don't tell me what I must do!' she snapped. 'And leave my father out of it!' She was being very rude, she knew, but this man brought out all the prickliness she hadn't felt since those bad old days when, in order to preserve her own identity, she had constantly opposed her father's orders. 'My father has nothing to do with it.'

The music stopped and he led her back to her table. But before he released her arm he spoke again, very low so that only she could hear. 'I'm very much afraid you'll find you're wrong about that.' And then, to Warren Martin, at the head of the table, 'Will you excuse me now, Warren? I have some work to get through tonight. Thank you for inviting me—I've enjoyed it very much. And I'll see you tomorrow—yes?'

Lucie looked at her father. His cheeks were flushed and his eyes slightly hazy. 'Yes, yes, tomorrow. Four o'clock at your office, we said, didn't we? Yes. Goodnight, Guy. Go carefully.'

Guy Devereux smiled at the company round the table. 'I always do,' he said quietly.

Lucie sank into her chair beside Peter. Her knees were shaking. She tried, and failed, to look away from Guy Devereux, so that she wouldn't see whether or not he was fixing his piercing blue gaze on her personally before he turned and walked away.

He was, and something in his eyes made her cringe all through her body. Don't be idiotic, she told herself. The man can't harm you in any way.

But as she watched him walk across the deck, so tall and formidable, and disappear behind the overhanging greenery, she felt a tightening in her stomach that was very like panic.

CHAPTER THREE

'TIRED, poppet?' Warren Martin parked the car and wrapped his arm around Lucie as they walked up the path to the villa, nestling under the coconut palms, ghostly white in the starlight.

'Mm, just a bit.' The breeze was cool on her hot forehead, and the lapping of the waves mingled lazily with the chirping of myriad night insects. It could have been a perfect evening if that man Devereux hadn't been at the party to spoil it.

Her father pushed open the door and switched on the lights. 'A pity we hadn't room to put Peter up at the villa here. He looked a bit gloomy to have to leave you.'

Yes, Peter had indeed looked gloomy when they parted. Never mind, she would make it up to him tomorrow. They would have a lovely day together.

Blossom had left a flask of coffee and a plate of sandwiches on the low table in the living-room, and Lucie sank into a chair and unscrewed the top from the flask. 'Coffee, Father?'

He was taking a bottle of whisky out of the drinks cupboard, but now he put it back again. 'Maybe I'd better opt for coffee,' he said ruefully. He came across the room and sat in the chair opposite. 'I probably overdid the wine at supper somewhat. I need a clear head if I'm to get up early in the morning to go diving with Steve.'

'Do you have to go diving?' queried Lucie. 'You look a bit tired.'

Warren Martin laughed heartily. 'Me, tired? You should know me better than that. I've never allowed myself more than four hours' sleep a night and I've got along very well on it. No, I'll be rarin' to go in the morning. The diving's great on the wall at Brac. When you go deep you're in another world, you forget all your worries.' For a moment a shadow passed over his face and then he was laughing again. 'And anyway, I can't let old Steve Maddox down. He's dead keen to sample the diving on Cayman Brac and it's the last chance he'll get. The Maddoxes are going home to Houston the day after tomorrow.'

'I'm sorry about that,' said Lucie. 'I'd have liked to know Dorothy better. She seemed a nice person. Oh well, about getting up early, you know best.'

Her father's eyes twinkled. 'I never thought I'd hear you say that again, poppet. I thought you'd given me up as a bad job.' He paused. 'But I never stopped hoping that one day we'd make up our differences, that you'd come back. And now here you are, a poised young woman, a successful author with a brilliant career ahead of you.'

'I hope so.' She raised crossed fingers.

Her father took the cup of coffee she handed him and leaned back in his easy chair. 'This is like old times, isn't it? Remember how we used to sit and talk when you were on holiday from school?'

'Yes, we did, didn't we?' He had never known the rebellion that had been gathering strength inside her then. He had been so satisfied that his word was law and that she was happy to do as he wanted. It wasn't until she left school and the clash about her wish to study art surfaced that things had gone really wrong.

He sighed heavily now. 'I was a selfish brute, Lucie, I know that now. I've found out the hard way, but I hope it isn't too late. I can't tell you how much it means to me to have you here. You won't want to rush away again, will you?'

'We thought—about a week, if that's OK with you. Peter has only a week's holiday owing to him, and I'm very busy working on my new book.'

'When are you planning to get married?'

'Oh, not yet,' Lucie said hastily. 'We've not been engaged long.'

He nodded in a satisfied way. 'Doesn't do to rush into these things. That was the mistake I made with Stephanie. God, that was a dead loss—in more ways than one. She married me for what she could get out of me and made my life hell until I called it a day. Once she'd got a massive settlement at the time of the divorce she married a Brazilian bandleader. Yes, it was a bad time.' His face was grim as he remembered.

'I'm sorry,' Lucie said. She *was* sorry—sorry for her father's loneliness, for the egotism that had made good relationships impossible. But he had changed, she was more and more certain of that.

'All my own fault,' he said gruffly. 'I should have let you go your own way about art school. But I hated the idea of you looking like one of those scruffy art students and marching about waving banners.'

Lucie giggled. 'I'm sure I never would. All I wanted to do was paint.'

'Yes,' her father mused. 'I was wrong about that.

Wrong about trying to get you and Guy Devereux together, too. I felt afterwards that if I hadn't tried so hard, if I'd left it to him to make the running, you might have made a go of it, the two of you.' He watched her closely. 'Don't you think so?'

Lucie shook her head. 'Never! No way. Guy Devereux's the last man in the world I'd ever have wanted to marry.' She was surprised at the vehemence of her own voice. It would have been better to laugh it off now, given the new feeling of understanding between her and her father.

Warren Martin looked thoughtful. 'You never really had time to get to know him, did you? He's a splendid chap, one of the best. And you know, he's never forgotten you. He was here the other day and he was asking me about you when he saw your picture over there.'

There didn't seem any answer to that, so Lucie was silent. Thank heaven for Peter, she thought. If she had arrived here free and unattached her father might well have started his matchmaking ploys again.

'Ah well, it's all water under the bridge now.' Warren Martin pulled himself to his feet. 'Bed for you, little girl, you look whacked. We shouldn't have stayed so late at The Waves' Edge, but everyone seemed to be having a good time.'

'Oh, they were. It was a lovely party.' After Guy Devereux left Lucie had resolutely entered into the spirit of the evening. She had danced with her father, with Peter, with the men guests. She had laughed and talked and drunk far more than she usually did, but now she was suddenly so tired that her eyelids were drooping. 'Yes, bed would be a good idea.' She yawned. 'Are you coming up?'

'Soon,' he said. 'Just one or two bits and pieces to clear up first.' He gestured towards the big rolltop desk in the corner of the room.

Lucie's smile was affectionate. 'You'll never learn to take it easy, will you?'

'Plenty of time to take it easy later on.' He pointed downwards significantly.

'Don't,' she pleaded. 'You've got lots and lots of time still.'

'Yes, of course, only a joke. Now, you go along, poppet, and have a lovely long sleep, and I'll see you when we get back from our dive tomorrow. Don't be surprised if you hear me go out again tonight—I usually take a stroll by the sea before I turn in.'

Then he did something he hadn't done for years. He put his arms round her and kissed her. She kissed him back and felt a quick pang as she noticed the way the skin of his cheek was falling into the loose folds of age. 'Good night, Father dear, it's lovely to be here with you,' she said softly, and took herself upstairs to fall asleep almost immediately, with the swish of the waves in her ears and the feeling of contentment that comes from the knowledge that a bitter quarrel has been happily made up.

She wakened to a light tap on the door and the sight of Blossom's wide smiling face appearing round it. 'Good morning, miss.' The maid came into the room and drew the curtains back.

'Good morning,' Lucie yawned and pulled herself

up in the bed. 'Goodness, I have slept! What time is it?'

'Twelve o'clock, Miss Martin. I'll be leaving soon—I work mornings and evenings here—and I thought you'd like breakfast before I go. I've brought you a tray up.'

She went to the landing and came back with a laden tray and placed it on Lucie's knees. 'There you are then, miss, I hope it's what you like. And a gentleman called about nine o'clock. He said not to wake you. He left a note for you.' Blossom fished in the capacious pocket of her overall and pulled out an envelope. 'Well, I'll be going then, miss, if there isn't anything more.'

'No, nothing, Blossom, and thank you for bringing my breakfast. It looks lovely.' The aroma of coffee and the sight of crisp rolls and butter and a selection of preserves was making Lucie's mouth water.

When Blossom had gone she poured out coffee and drank a whole cup before she opened Peter's note. Poor old Peter, he must have been up early. She hoped he hadn't been too bored wandering around by himself while she slept.

She had to read the note through twice before it began to make any sense at all.

'My dear Lucie,' Peter had scrawled, 'Forgive me, but something has come up unexpectedly, which means that I have to go back to London immediately, catching an early flight. You've made it up with your father, so my useful role here is over. I hoped you might fall for me, but if you had we'd have made love long before this, book or no book, as I think you'll agree. And I saw your face when you

were dancing with Devereux last night and that told
me the lot. We'll meet again as friends when you
come back to London, I very much hope. Yours as
always, Peter.'

Very slowly she refolded the note and replaced it
in the envelope. She drank a second cup of coffee,
but her appetite had gone. Peter was right, of course,
she didn't love him; all her plans had been selfish
ones.

She showered and dressed, feeling upset and
guilty. But as she walked out into the sunshine and
down to the edge of the crystal-clear water and felt
the light breeze on her face, she began to cheer up.
Peter wasn't heart-broken, he wasn't the type. He
would find another girl who would really care for
him and not put her own wishes and ambitions first.
Really, he was well rid of her, she thought wryly.

As for the bit about seeing her face when she was
dancing with Guy Devereux—that was a joke. What
Peter had taken for passion had been just that—but
it had been the passion of anger, not of love. Peter
could hardly have been more mistaken. If—when—
they met again as friends she would tell him that, and
they might even laugh about it together.

For the best part of an hour she sat on the warm
white sand at the edge of the water, hugging her
knees, absently watching the black snorkel tubes
bobbing up and down like cormorants, and the tiny
bodies of the water-skiers, far out beyond the reef,
where the colour of the sea darkened, leaning back
on their ropes behind the buzzing speedboats. Until
at last she noticed that she seemed to have Seven
Mile Beach almost to herself and realised that

everyone had gone back to their villas and condos
and hotels for lunch and siesta, and that she herself
was hungry.

Realised, too, as she made her way indoors again,
that her principal feeling was one of relief, and
gratitude to Peter for seeing the truth about their
relationship and taking matters into his own hands.

Except for the coffee, the breakfast-tray that
Blossom had prepared was untouched. Lucie made
more coffee in the immaculate small kitchen, found
cheese and fruit to add to the tray and carried it into
the living-room. Here she made a very hearty lunch
and then lay back in an easy chair in front of the
open window to wait for her father's return. He had
said that his appointment was for four o'clock. He
hadn't said what time he expected to get back to the
villa, but she was quite content to wait.

The fan whirred gently on the ceiling and the
canopy over the verandah kept the heat of the sun
from the room. It was very quiet, except for the cries
of a group of children playing on the sands and the
lazy splash of the waves and the occasional squawk
of sea-birds. Lucie closed her eyes and began to
picture her next book.

It was a coincidence that she should have thought
of tropical fish. Now she had her models right here in
the lagoon. There were so many of them, with such
wonderful names—angelfish, butterfly fish, squirrel
fish, grunts—she remembered those from the last
holiday she had spent here. The colours would be a
real joy to paint—yellow and blue and red and black,
striped and plain. And the coral! Fabulous colours
and shapes! Lucie closed her eyes and began to drift

away into a dreamy state, half awake, half asleep, seeing the whole book gradually taking shape in her mind's eye.

'Lucie!

She started, blinking herself awake at the sound of a deep voice from behind her chair. Not her father's voice, certainly. Turning her head, she saw the tall figure of Guy Devereux standing in the doorway and felt that familiar tweak of something like fear in the pit of her stomach.

'I apologise for walking in like this, there was no answer to my knock.' He wasn't smiling, and his thick-lashed blue eyes were fixed on her face in the way that always made her feel weak at the knees.

She jumped up, putting a hand on the back of the chair to steady herself. 'You've come to see my father? I'm afraid he's not here at present.'

'I see. When he didn't turn up for our appointment I thought perhaps there'd been a misunderstanding, so I came along to see if we could have our consultation here.'

'I'm sorry,' she said flatly, 'I can't help you.'

'Do you know where he is?' He shot the question at her as if—she thought resentfully—she were in the witness box.

'He flew to Cayman Brac early this morning with friends, that's all I can tell you.' Now go away, she willed him. Just turn round and walk out.

But he didn't move, and they stood there looking at each other in silence across the width of the room. This is ridiculous, Lucie thought, I can't very well make him go, and I'm certainly not going to ask him to stay.

The sound of the telephone cut through the silence. Lucie went across to the desk in the corner of the room and lifted the receiver, her back to Guy Devereux. Surely he would take the hint now and go away. He could hardly stay and listen to what must be a personal conversation.

'Hello—hello—is that Miss Lucie Martin?'

'Yes,' said Lucie, not recognising the voice.

'This is Steven Maddox, ringing from Cayman Brac. Miss Martin, is your fiancé there with you?'

'No. No, he isn't here at present.' What on earth did Steve Maddox want with Peter?

'Well, is there anyone else with you? Are you alone?'

She glanced over her shoulder. Guy Devereux was still standing in the doorway, damn him. 'No, I'm not alone. Mr Devereux is here at the moment,' she said coldly. 'Is there a message from my father? Can I——?'

'Would you ask Mr Devereux to speak to me?'

Suddenly she was aware of the strain in Steve Maddox's voice. Something was wrong. Dumbly she held out the receiver to Guy and he came quickly across the room and took it from her.

She sank back into her chair, watching his face as he listened, trying to make out words from the other end of the line, but it was merely a faint unrecognisable mutter.

Finally Guy said in an odd voice, 'Yes, I'll deal with it. I'll be here until you get back.'

He replaced the receiver and came and stood in front of Lucie's chair, looking down at her silently.

Her fingers dug into the soft velvet arms of the

chair. 'Something's wrong,' she said. 'My father?'

He pulled up a small chair and sat down beside her so that their heads were on a level. 'There's been a diving accident,' he said.

She didn't have to ask, she saw it in his face, but she said flatly, 'He's dead, isn't he?'

'I'm sorry,' Guy said, and leaned towards her, covering her hand strongly with his.

Afterwards she wondered why she didn't resent his touch and pull away. But at the time all she thought was how glad she was that she had come, that she and her father had had this little time to heal their wounds together.

She shivered, and Guy got up and poured out a glass of brandy. 'Thank you,' she said. 'I just feel— cold.'

He nodded. 'I know. Shock.' He went away and came back with her white woollen jacket and draped it over her shoulders. She clutched it round her with one hand and held the brandy with the other. Her teeth chattered against the glass as she drank.

She coughed as the spirit stung her throat, and he took the empty glass from her and said, 'Stick your arms in the sleeves.' One at a time he lifted her arms and eased them into the sleeves of the jacket, as if she were a three-year-old.

She said, 'I'm all right now. What did Steve say?'

'Not very much. He was diving with your father and he checked all the gear carefully before they went down, as diving-partners always do. He thinks—at a guess—that it must have been a sudden thing, a stroke perhaps, or a coronary.'

She nodded and they were both silent. Then she

said, 'What must I do?'

'Where's your fiancé? He'll take over for you, I'm sure.'

She shook her head. 'Peter's gone. He had to go back to England. He flew out early this morning.' She passed a hand distractedly across her forehead. 'James—I must get James.'

'James?'

'My brother. I must let him know what's happened.'

'Of course. You can contact him?'

'Yes, he's in Birmingham.' She stopped. 'Oh heavens, no, he isn't!' Suddenly everything seemed impossibly difficult. 'He's in Europe—he said behind the Iron Curtain, but I don't know where. I'll have to telephone his office in Birmingham and see if they can get in touch with him.'

There was a moment or two of silence, then Guy said, 'Look, suppose you leave everything to me—until your brother can get here? For a start I'll phone his Birmingham office if you'll give me the number.'

She bit her lip. She had thought this man hard, unfeeling, and here he was offering help just when she most needed it. 'Thank you,' she said, 'you're being very kind.' She gave him the number and he jotted it down in a notebook. She had a stupid idea of apologising to him for being so rude last night, but before she could think of any way of doing it there was a knock on the door and Dorothy Maddox came into the room, her plump pink face the picture of sympathy under its crown of wavy white hair.

She flew across the room and sank on to the floor beside Lucie, taking both her hands. 'Steve just phoned me. Oh, you poor dear,' she crooned, 'I'm so, so sorry. You must be absolutely shattered!' She glanced around the room. 'Your fiancé—is he with you?'

Guy answered for her. 'He's left,' he said shortly. 'Had to return to the UK.'

'Oh, that's bad, that sure is bad. Well, you must let me look after you. Come along to our villa next door and you can rest.' She was all maternal caring, her eyes misty with tears.

Lucie looked pleadingly towards Guy and even as she did so she thought with terrible wryness, so much for my wonderful independence, but I can't handle this myself, I can't. Save me from Dorothy, she willed him. I can't take a lot of understanding and sympathy.

But he merely nodded. 'Good idea, I'll know where to find you, then. I'll be along as soon as I have anything to report.'

Lucie let Dorothy lead her out of the room. She would have preferred to stay with Guy, extraordinary though that might have seemed a short time ago. His calm, dispassionate manner was just what she needed. She was still partly in shock, but she was dimly aware that her feelings were a long way away from straightforward grief at the death of a beloved parent. The situation between her father and herself had been too fraught, too complex for that.

But Dorothy was tactful as well as kind. She installed Lucie on a sofa and covered her legs with a fleecy rug and made her drink sweet tea. 'You've had a bad shock, you poor thing, and you must keep very quiet. I'll sit here by you and you can talk if you feel

ike it, but it would be better if you could just close
your eyes and shut everything out and have a little
sleep. Just swallow these tablets—they'll help.'

Lucie obediently swallowed the tablets and after a
while began to feel drowsy. After that everything
became very vague—the tablets must have been
stronger than she had expected. Time ceased to
register. From somewhere a long way away she
heard voices and knew that she was being discussed.
A man's voice said, 'OK, I'll carry her up,' and she
was being lifted in strong arms and carried upstairs
and lowered gently on to a cool bed. A hand stroked
her hair gently back from her face and the same deep
voice said, 'Everything's all right, Lucie, I'll look
after you.'

James, she thought, it must be James, he must
have got here very quickly. Dear James, he was such
a comfort. She tried to open her eyes, but the lids
seemed glued together. She reached up and drew his
head down and rubbed her cheek against his. 'Don't
leave me,' she murmured.

'I'll never leave you,' he said, and that seemed a
funny thing for James to say. She wanted to ask
about Angela, and if things were all right between
them, but she was too tired to find the words.
Everything was dim and confused, as if there were a
fog enclosing her. She sighed deeply and was asleep.

She woke with the feeling of a huge lump in the
region of her chest, making breathing difficult.
Sunlight was filtering through the drawn curtains
and she lay still and stared at the bright patterns on
the ceiling, and gradually she remembered all that

had happened—up to the time that Dorothy had given her the tablets.

She felt terrible. Her mouth was dry and her head was heavy and achy. She was wearing only bra and pants—her cotton dress was hanging over the back of a chair; Dorothy must have taken it off at some time.

She must get up and wash and dress and then she could face the day and everything that had to be done. She slid out of bed and staggered into the adjoining bathroom. When she had swilled her face and tidied her hair with a comb she found on the bathroom shelf she felt marginally better. She shook out the cotton dress and put it on again. Her white fleecy coat was on the chair too, and she remembered that Guy Devereux had found it and put it on for her after the telephone call.

He had promised to look after everything for her, and she remembered how in the weakness of the moment she had agreed. But of course she couldn't let him, she must handle things herself until James arrived.

Until James arrived! But James was *here*! Dimly, she remembered him putting his arms round her and kissing her last night, and she had clung to him.

She sank into a chair, trying to make sense out of that. Of course James wasn't here—there was no way he could possibly have got here in the time. Then who had carried her upstairs—comforted and kissed her so tenderly? Steve, she thought, that nice teddy-bear of a man. Yes, it must have been Dorothy's Steve. Otherwise—but she refused to believe that it had been Guy Devereux. The very idea made her go hot all over.

The door opened and Dorothy's face appeared round it, drawn into anxious lines. 'Oh, you're awake, Lucie, and you've got up! Now that surely is a relief.' She came further into the room, one hand on her breast which was rising and falling nervously. 'I've been out of my mind with worry, and Steve's been so mad at me for giving you those tablets. The doctor gave them to me to settle me down when I'd had my operation and couldn't sleep, and I brought them away with me. But Steve said you should never give your medicines to anyone else—and Guy said he'd given you brandy before and that made it more dangerous—and you passed out like a light and——' Her fingers twined themselves together in agitation. 'If I'd harmed you I'd never have forgiven myself—if you hadn't been awake I was going to try to find a doctor——'

Lucie stood up and put her hand on Dorothy's arm. 'Please don't. I'm perfectly all right, and I'm sure that when you've had a shock the best thing is to sleep until you can pull yourself together. Now don't worry any more about it, will you?'

Dorothy leaned forward and kissed her. 'You're a sweet girl,' she said hurriedly, 'and we want to help as much as we can, but Steve *has* to go back to Houston tomorrow because of his business. He'll have to come back later, of course, to give evidence, but meanwhile Guy has taken everything over and he's being just marvellous, attending to all the legal things. He's waiting downstairs, to see you. I said I'd join Steve in the town—he went to interview the

Governor about us leaving tomorrow.' She clicked
her tongue distractedly. 'Oh dear, it's all so difficult!'

Legal things! Of course! Lucie closed her eyes as
her head began to swim. Her mind shrank from the
prospect of all the rather ghastly enquiries that must
follow an accidental death. And all the things she
ought to try to deal with until James arrived! There
must be officals to interview, forms to sign. She
wasn't sure if she could handle it, but she would have
to try.

She drew in a deep breath. 'I'll come down,' she
said. 'Please tell Guy I'll join him in a few minutes.'

Dorothy got to her feet, looking vastly relieved.
'That's arranged, then. I'll leave you and Guy
together to talk.'

She bustled away, and Lucie waited until she
heard the car start up, then she squared her shoulders
and went downstairs to face Guy Devereaux.

He was on the verandah, leaning his elbows on the
rail and staring out over the sea. He hadn't heard her
and she stopped for a moment, fighting down the
sinking feeling in the pit of her stomach at the sight
of him, so big and male and overwhelming.

'Good morning,' she said in a small voice.

He straightened up and turned immediately. He
was wearing very dark-grey trousers and an open-
necked shirt to match this morning. Perhaps he was
in mourning for her father, Lucie thought idiotically.
'Hello, Lucie, it's good to see you up. How are you
feeling?'

'I'm fine,' she said automatically.

He looked hard at her pale face. 'Hm—well, that's
as may be. Come and sit down out here, it's cool on

he verandah. The maid's just brought you some
breakfast.'

Lucie could only nibble at the crisp rolls, but the
coffee was good and strong and the bowl of fruit
tempting. Guy sat on the opposite side of the small
cane table and poured the coffee.

'What's happened?' she asked him. 'Have you
been able to contact James?'

He shook his head. 'I got through to the number in
Birmingham that you gave me, but his office there
haven't heard from him since he left for Bulgaria. He
promised to contact them as soon as he knew where
he was going to stay. They're expecting to hear from
him at any moment and then, of course, they'll pass
on the message and he'll get in touch. I gave them the
number of my office here, I thought that would be
the best.'

Lucie's heart sank; she had been banking on
James being told immediately what had happened,
on his arriving soon, perhaps within twenty-four
hours. But now everything seemed frighteningly
vague. She took a sip of coffee and said, 'Thank you
for what you've done, but I really mustn't trouble you
any further. I expect James will telephone later today
and I can handle things myself until he can get here.'

Guy leaned back, dark brows raised. 'Have you
any idea at all of all the formalities that will have to
be gone through? Have you any experience at all of a
situation like this? Do you really think you're
capable of handling it?—because frankly I don't.'

She bit back an indignant retort. It was no use
kidding herself that she didn't need help—she
needed help very badly indeed until James could get

here. 'I expect I could get advice from—from the authorities here.'

'Look,' he said patiently, 'I've offered my help, why not accept it?'

'Because——' she began. Because you frighten me. There's something about you that disturbs me so that I can't think straight. Something about the way you look at me. 'I—I don't know,' she muttered. 'I'm not very good at accepting help.'

'Well, it's time you began to learn, then,' he said crisply. 'Now just forget about the—arrangements that have to be made. I'll see the officials concerned and find out the regulations and inform them that your brother will be arriving shortly. That should cover things for the moment.' He was watching her closely as he added, 'As the Caymans are British, I assume that there'll have to be an inquest, as there would at home.'

'Yes,' Lucie said tonelessly.

There was a long silence, then he said gently, 'Lucie, do you care very much?'

She stared at him wide-eyed. 'H-how dare you suggest——' she burst out. 'That's a beastly insinuation! Of course I care. He was my father—of course I care. And what's it got to do with you, anyway?'

'I had to ask you,' he said, 'for reasons that will become clear later on. You see, I happen to know a little of what happened between you and your father. As his banker I've been in touch with him on and off ever since you quarrelled with him and walked out. I know that you haven't seen him again until you arrived here—yesterday, wasn't it?'

'You seem to be very well informed, Mr Devereux

Or do you employ a private investigator to watch your customers and pry into their affairs? I imagine that's the way big business operates, isn't it? Well, there are a few things you don't know. My father and I made up our quarrel and I was so—so very happy that things were right between us again. I was looking forward to—to——' she bit her lip as tears stung behind her eyes. 'And now he's gone—it—it's horrible!'

She turned away, covering her face as sobs shook her. After a few moments a folded handkerchief was thrust into her hand. She mopped her eyes, gulping. 'Sorry,' she muttered.

'It's I who should be sorry,' Guy Devereux said formally. 'Please accept my apology. I had no right to say what I did.' He reached across the table and took the handkerchief from her.

There was an awkward little silence—at least, it was awkward for Lucie. As for the man sitting opposite, she got the impression that he would never feel awkward, at a loss, under any circumstances. When she couldn't bear the silence any longer she said in a muffled voice, 'I've been silly, I suppose. I try to be too independent. I'd be glad of your help until James arrives.'

'Good,' he said shortly. 'That's sensible of you. I'll let you know immediately I have word of your brother. Meanwhile, I'll be in touch with the authorities and give them any information they need at this stage. You just take it easy for the moment—stay with Dorothy and Steve while they're here—they're pleasant people.'

'Yes,' she said. It was just like it had been before—

a man taking charge of everything, telling her what to do, expecting her to obey him. Guy Devereux was—as her father had been—a dominant male, and that was all there was to it. She comforted herself with the thought that it wasn't for long, that James would soon be here and then everything would be different.

'I'll leave you, then. Try to eat some breakfast— and there's plenty of coffee still in the pot.' He walked round and stood beside her chair. 'I'll be back later on and we'll have dinner somewhere quiet. There's a great deal I have to discuss with you, Lucie.' He put a hand briefly on her shoulder. 'Goodbye for the present.'

She watched him walk away along the verandah, so tall and strong and so maddeningly in control of himself and everything else. *Could* she have stood out against him? she wondered. *Could* she have snubbed him and refused his help? For all sorts of reasons the answer was No, she couldn't. She had to accept that for the moment she had to be what he called 'sensible'—which meant that she had to do as she was told. She put a hand to her shoulder where his hand had touched it, and suddenly she was reliving that moment in the garden in Paris, three years ago, when she had been eighteen. A long shudder passed through her as she remembered the feel of his lips, his hands. It hadn't only been her shoulder he had touched then, and the way her body had responded had terrified her. Nothing like it had happened to her since, she had taken care of that.

She stood up and shook herself impatiently, then she walked across the soft sand to the water's edge and stood there trying to sort out her thoughts and feelings. But it was all too much and it had happened too quickly, and the waves breaking lazily at her feet supplied no answer.

She was still standing there when Steve and Dorothy returned, and the question that was filling her mind was what Guy had meant when he said he had a great deal to discuss with her. Somehow that had an ominous ring about it. Oh, James, she thought desperately, why aren't you here?

CHAPTER FOUR

LUCIE was sitting alone on the verandah of the
Maddoxes' villa when Guy came back that evening.
It had been a strange afternoon. She had stayed with
the Maddoxes, not, she assured herself, because Guy
had told her to, but because she couldn't yet face the
prospect of returning to her father's villa next door.
Dorothy—that understanding soul—had been there
and brought back Lucie's clothes and toilet things.
'Until you decide what you're going to do,' she said.

Lucie thanked her and said she must go back to
the villa tomorrow. Indeed, she had no choice. Even
if she could get a room at a hotel the cost would be ten
times as much as she could afford. But it was good to
have her clothes here and it was good to get out of the
cotton dress she had worn yesterday through all the
confusion.

'Make free with the bathroom and everything,'
Dorothy urged her, and she accepted the invitation
gladly. When she had showered she put on the
second of the two cotton dresses she had brought
with her. Beach-wear seemed out of place today, and
the dress was simple and pretty and unassuming, a
crisp peach-coloured cotton with white polka dots
and narrow shoulder-straps. Quite appropriate for a
dinner with Guy Devereux to talk business, so she
wouldn't have to go to the bother of changing again
this evening. She would take trouble with her hair

78

and her make-up, she decided, but she had no intention of dressing up for his benefit.

The day was hot and there was a suspended, unreal quality about it. Lucie's mind recoiled from thinking about what had happened but, fortunately, Dorothy was a compulsive talker and in her company you didn't have to think. Lucie helped her with her packing, listened to Dorothy's stories of her grandchildren and talked a little of her own two nieces, and they drank long, cool drinks and ate cookies while Steve spent most of the afternoon telephoning his office in New York. After one slightly embarrassed remark that it was such a shame that Lucie's fiancé hadn't been here, Dorothy didn't refer to Peter again. Lucie had the idea that she suspected that something might have gone wrong.

Steve and Dorothy went out for a meal just before seven. Before they left Dorothy called at the next-door villa to tell Blossom, the maid, what had happened. 'She hadn't got around to cooking the meal, so that was OK. She says she's very sorry about your father; and she'll call here tomorrow to find out what you need. She's a good girl, she really was quite upset. You'll be OK on your own until Guy arrives?' Dorothy went on rather anxiously. 'Steve says he thinks Guy planned to go over to Cayman Brac this afternoon, but he should be back later on this evening. Anyway, if he doesn't turn up we won't be away long.'

But he did turn up, of course. Guy Devereux would come if he said he would come, Lucie was confident of that. If she had to rely on the man it was, she supposed, lucky that he was the reliable type. She felt the by-now-familiar little tug inside as she saw him walking purposefully along the verandah towards her, looking, as usual, extremely impressive in a pale lightweight suit. It was annoying that the man should have this purely physical effect on her, but there was nothing she could do about it. Some men, she knew, exuded sex appeal effortlessly, and they were not always the most admirable men. You admitted that and were on your guard against it—if you had any sense, or any self-respect. The chemistry could be recognised and then ignored.

'You all alone?' he queried, without any other greeting. 'Let's get going, then. We'll have dinner at my hotel, it's not too touristy and reasonably quiet.'

He led the way out to his car and Lucie picked up her handbag and white fleecy jacket and followed—like a little poodle, she thought resentfully. But not for long, Mr Guy Devereux. Oh no, not for long. And if that makes me an ungrateful beast, so be it.

The hotel was a short drive from the Maddoxes' villa, a long, low building fronted by masses of brightly-coloured flowers. The dining-room was still almost empty and the diners already there looked like extremely affluent businessmen. Lucie was familiar with the type. Tourism and money were the two faces of the Caymans, and this was the money face. Even Guy was wearing a tie this evening—silk, with a Paisley pattern, and Lucie had to admit reluctantly that he was by far the most distinguished-looking man in the room.

He was greeted by one or two of the other diners as they were escorted to a table in a corner, and Lucie was conscious of the glances of the men and was glad she had taken some trouble with her appearance. She intended to hold her own in every way with Guy, and that included looking presentable on the very few occasions when she had to be in his company.

'What do you fancy?' he asked, when the waiter had produced the large bill of fare. 'Fish? Fish? Or—er—possibly fish?'

Wonders would never cease! He had actually made a joke—of sorts. Lucie remembered that fish was always the principal item in Cayman Island cuisine—and very delicious it was, too. 'I couldn't ask for anything I'd like better than lobster,' she said. 'And aren't you being a little unfair? There *are* other things on the menu.'

'Possibly. But I'm very often unfair, as you'll find out when you know me better.' There was a glint in the dark-blue eyes that searched hers lazily.

It was incredible, he was actually trying to flirt with her—now, of all times. How insensitive could you get? 'I doubt if I shall need to do more than accept your help for the moment, until my brother gets here,' she said coldly. 'So there'll hardly be time to get to know you better.'

He rubbed his cheek thoughtfully. 'I wonder why you hate me so much, Lucie.' As the wine-waiter approached he added, 'Ah well, it will doubtless all be revealed in due course—*when we know each other better*,' he repeated with maddening complacency.

Afterwards, Lucie remembered very little of the dinner they ate. She was keyed up and on her guard with Guy, who seemed to be in a very strange mood—one minute treating her to his own brand of

humour—which was too ironic for her taste—and
the next concentrating on his food with a withdrawn,
stern expression. He had said they had things to
discuss, and she waited for him to start the
discussion.

Before they had finished their coffee the dining-
room had filled up and Guy was obviously impatient
to be gone. 'We can't talk here,' he said. 'We'll go up
to my room.' He glanced sideways at her as he signed
the check. 'Don't be alarmed, Lucie, I'm not
suggesting anything improper.' He made it sound as
if she were some Victorian miss, she thought angrily.
But wasn't that exactly how she had behaved that
night in the garden in Paris, when she had pushed
him into the rose-bed and run away? She glanced at
the lean, dark face and the straight mouth. It would
be madness to tangle with a man who packed such an
alarming sexual punch. Better to leave that to the
girls in his own league—of whom there were no
doubt plenty.

'I'm not in the least alarmed.' She lifted her chin as
they went up the stairs, and she was fairly sure that
he was smiling his hateful, ironic smile.

His room was of moderate size and comfortably
furnished in dark wood. 'I usually stay here when I
come to the Caymans,' he said conversationally,
drawing the red damask curtains. 'It's what you
might call a family hotel—very friendly. Do sit
down.' He pulled out a small basket-chair for her.
'Would you like anything more to drink? I have a
small store here.' He slid open a door in the wall-
fitment.

'No, thank you,' Lucie said politely.

'Well, I hope you don't mind if I do.' He poured himself a whisky and came and sat down on the other basket-chair, which looked much too small for him.

He took a swig of whisky and set the glass down on the floor. 'Lucie——' he began, and stopped. 'I don't know how to tell you this.'

The blood drained from her cheeks as an appalling thought struck her. 'James? Has something happened to James? Tell me—quickly——'

He shook his head impatiently. 'No, nothing like that. I haven't heard from your brother yet,' he said, and Lucie slumped back in her chair, releasing her breath.

When he spoke again he seemed to be choosing his words carefully. 'You know, perhaps, that your father was one of my bank's customers. Has been for some time. Over the years we've helped him with a considerable amount of finance.' He paused. 'Would I be right in thinking that you're not very well up in business matters?'

'You'd be quite right. If it's something to do with business and it concerns me, please spell it out in words of one syllable.'

'That's not easy, the situation is complicated. But to make it as simple as possible I'm afraid I must tell you that your father is—was—on the verge of bankruptcy. Things have been happening recently in his various companies that have made it impossible for the bank to go on advancing money to him any longer.'

Lucie stared at him, her brow wrinkled. 'But—but he'd have put things right. He's been through difficult times before and he's always come out on top at the end.'

'Not this time, I'm afraid.'

'What does it mean?' she asked, white-faced.

'It means that all his companies will have to be wound up—go out of business.'

'All of them?' she whispered, and she thought: What about James—and Angela—and the girls?

'All of them.'

Lucie's hands curled themselves into tight balls. It was too much—on top of everything else. But she must get it clear. 'Does that—would that include the company my brother James manages in England, too?'

'I'm afraid so.'

'But it's not fair!' Her voice rose in desperation. 'James's company is doing well, he told me so only a few days ago.' She remembered James saying he needed more capital and that their father was being obstructive, but she didn't mention that to this man sitting there grim-faced, like a judge pronouncing sentence.

He shrugged. 'Possibly. But it looks as if all your father's companies were, so to speak, mixed up together in a devil's brew. If one goes, they all go.'

Lucie began to shake inside. 'There must be some way out,' she muttered. 'There *must*!' James mustn't be faced with this. 'Oh, isn't there something you could do?' She looked up pleadingly into the hard face of the man sitting opposite.

He said slowly, 'There might be a way, if you cared to take it.'

'Oh, please tell me.' She clasped her hands

ogether. 'If you could help I'd be eternally grateful.
James has worked so hard and built up the business,
and he's such a—such a *reliable* person. And he's
devoted to Angela, his wife, and they have two lovely
little girls——'

The words died away as she saw the look on his
face. She wasn't making any impression—he wasn't
the type to allow his actions to be influenced by any
appeal to his feelings. Always supposing that he had
any feelings about anything except money, she
thought bitterly. He probably hadn't even heard her
emotional appeal.

But she was wrong, he *had* heard. 'You care a good
deal about your brother and his family?'

Her eyes flashed indignantly. 'Of course I care.
They're my *family*!'

He nodded. 'Then that might make my proposal
more acceptable to you.'

'W-what do you mean?'

The probing, blue eyes under their fringe of dark
lashes regarded her with an almost hypnotic gaze. 'I
mean,' he said, 'that if I were involved with the
rescue of your brother's company *as a family matter*
then the situation would be entirely different. I could
do all that would be necessary to keep your brother's
company viable.'

Lucie licked her dry lips. 'But I don't see—how
could it be a family matter? You're not family.'

'I would be. If you and I were married.'

'Married?' She stared at him, glassy-eyed. 'But
that's impossible! We hardly know each other and
we're—we're not in love. Quite the reverse, in fact,'
she added bitterly. 'You're not serious?'

'Dead serious,' he said, and she saw that he was. The dazzling blue eyes held her own until she had to look away. Didn't he ever blink? she wondered dazedly.

She drew in a deep breath and looked back, and he was still staring at her as if he were learning her face by heart. Heart? What was she thinking of? A man like Guy Devereux didn't deal in hearts, only in pounds and dollars.

'Is there—could I have a drink, please?'

'Of course.' He was on his feet immediately. 'Whisky—sherry—brandy?'

'I think,' she said weakly, 'that brandy is indicated. A small one, please.'

He poured the drink, and as he handed it to her his fingers brushed hers and it was like an electric charge passing along her arms and down through her body.

He picked up his own glass and raised it towards her. 'I hope,' he said, without a glimmer of a smile, 'that we can toast our mutual pledge and understanding.'

Lucie took a gulp of the brandy and waited while it burned its way down her throat. Dutch courage, they called it, but any sort of courage would do at the moment. 'We certainly can't pledge anything,' she said, pleased that her voice sounded fairly steady. 'It's quite out of the question, as I said, and anyway, had you forgotten that I'm already engaged to be married?'

'Not any more, I think,' Guy said smoothly.

'Wh-what do you mean?' she stammered.

'Merely that your fiancé—your ex-fiancé—was

staying at this hotel last night and we had a drink together. He got quite confidential. Don't pretend to be heart-broken, Lucie, you weren't in love with him. I only had to look at the two of you together to see that.'

She went hot with anger. 'You—you——' She couldn't think of anything bad enough to call him. She gripped the stem of her brandy glass and lifted her arm, but his hand closed over it before she could throw the brandy in his complacent face.

'No need for hysteria,' he said with maddening calmness. 'I know you've been through a good deal in the last twenty-four hours, but losing your cool won't help.'

'Cool!' She flung the word at him. 'How can I be cool when the world is erupting like a volcano all round me? And you, sitting there making extra-ordinary suggestions that—that make no sense at all and just make me more confused and—and worried and——' She bit her lip hard as tears stung behind her eyelids. 'And take your hand off me! She wriggled her arm out of his grasp and sank back in her chair, closing her eyes, shivering with strain and fatigue.

His deep controlled voice came to her through a faint buzzing in her ears. 'I'm sorry, Lucie—believe me, I don't mean to hurt you. But we've got to talk sensibly and not let emotions run riot.'

He dared to talk of emotions! She kept her eyes tightly closed and she was afraid she was going to pass out. But she had to humour him, to keep this incredible conversation going. He had it in his power to save James's company, and if there was anything

she could do—short of his preposterous suggestion—
then she must find out what it was.

She drew in a deep breath. 'What have you in
mind, then, if I accept your terms?' She would have
liked to say 'blackmail', but she must avoid
antagonising him if she possibly could.

He seemed to relax slightly. He leaned back in his
chair. 'If you were my wife it would make your
brother's company my personal concern. If my
fellow-directors agreed—and I'm pretty sure they
would—we could work something out that would
save the company and allow it to continue as at
present. Your brother would be manager, as he is
now, but the bank would own the company. Also, I
think—hope—that it might be possible to avoid the
whole matter going to the courts.'

'The courts?' Lucie's eyes widened in disbelief.
'Are you trying to tell me that my father has been—
been stealing?'

'That isn't a word we use much in our line of
business,' Guy said evenly. 'Your father was a clever
man; he owned several companies, as I expect you
know. There are rules and regulations in company
law and I'm afraid he has recently been—how shall I
put it?—bending the rules somewhat. I learnt from
him when I came out here to see him that he's been
under considerable financial strain to meet a divorce
settlement, and probably because of that he appears
to have been using company funds for his personal
needs. Also transferring capital from one company
to another in ways that are almost certainly illegal,
although this has still to be sorted out by the lawyers.'

While he had been speaking Lucie's whole body

seemed to have been congealing into a block of ice. This was a nightmare, it couldn't be happening!

But somehow her mind went on working automatically. 'And if I agree to your proposal you can—so to speak—hush things up?'

He grimaced. 'It's not a sure thing, but I'd try my damnedest, and I believe I could. Certainly I could promise to extricate your brother's company. Possibly even the other companies could be saved in the long run.'

'But if I don't agree?'

He shrugged. 'Then I'm afraid matters would have to take their course. Unless I have some lever to use with my co-directors they wouldn't be interested. There would be a legal wrangle that might go on for years. Bankruptcies, redundancies, the name of Warren Martin a target for the press. They'd make a meal of it—"Millionaire escapes arrest. Warren Martin drowns in tax-haven".'

'Oh, that's cruel!' Lucie winced as if he had stuck a sharp blade through her.

'You have to face the truth,' he said implacably. 'And life can be very cruel.'

'Yes,' she said dully, 'I'm beginning to find that out.' She looked into the hard, arrogant face. 'Why do you want to marry me?' she asked.

For a second she thought he looked taken aback. But only for a second. Then he smiled faintly and the dark-blue eyes glittered between narrowed lids. 'I suppose you wouldn't believe me if I told you that I fell headlong in love with you that night in Paris, three years ago, and that I've been in love with you ever since?'

'No,' she said icily, 'I wouldn't believe you.' How could any man joke about such a painful, heart-breaking situation?

'Well then, let's see if I can put it more objectively. Marriage is something I've been considering recently. I'm thirty-four. When my father retired last year I became chairman of the bank and my life-style has inevitably changed somewhat.' His lip twisted. 'I have had to become, like it or not, a more solid citizen, with all that goes with that status. And that seems to include a beautiful and poised wife.' The blue eyes passed over her slowly, and she cringed inside. 'You seem to fit the bill, Lucie Martin.'

She fought down her humiliation and despair. 'Why not one of your girl-friends?—I'm sure you have plenty who would be delighted to fit the bill, as you call it. Why choose a girl who—who dislikes you as much as I do?'

He smiled hatefully. 'A little dislike can be very alluring.' He paused, his eyes passing downwards to fix themselves on her soft breasts, rising and falling with barely-suppressed rage and despair under her thin cotton dress. 'I think we'd be very good together, Lucie. You might even fall in love with me in time.'

She didn't try to keep the contempt out of her voice as she said, 'I could never fall in love with you. You represent everything that I loathe and detest. There, is that plain enough? Do you still want to marry me?'

'Certainly,' he said.

Lucie never knew how she managed to get through

that horrible night. 'Think it over,' Guy Devereux
had said when he drew the car up in front of the
Maddoxes' villa. 'I'll be along to see you in the
morning and you must give me your decision then.
We can't hang about in a matter like this. I should
think that your brother will be in touch some time
tomorrow and we must get this settled before he
arrives.' He switched off the engine and in the faint
light from the inside of the villa she saw his mouth
curve into that faint ironic smile that set her teeth on
edge as he asked, 'I take it you won't want him to be
aware of the great and noble sacrifice you're making
on his behalf?'

'*If* I decide to make it,' she said tonelessly. By then
she had been too tired even to argue with him.

'Oh, I think you will,' he said. 'And I'll do my best
to make sure that it's not too much of a sacrifice.
Anyway, sleep on it. Good night, Lucie.' He seemed
to hesitate before he added, 'I'm sorry it's been such
a rotten day for you.'

She thought his tone had softened, but the last
thing she wanted from him was pity. She needed to
go on thinking of him as ruthless, hard, dominating,
all the things she hated in a man.

He moved towards her and she panicked. He was
going to kiss her and it mustn't happen. 'Good
night,' she muttered, turning her head away and
fumbling with the door handle. As she stumbled out
of the car and up the path to the villa she heard the
sound of his soft, mocking laughter.

The Maddoxes were catching the eight-fifteen
flight to Miami, and Lucie was only too glad to be up
early to see them off. Dorothy kissed her with tears

in her eyes. 'I hate leaving you, you poor dear, and I do hope your brother will get here soon. Steve will probably have to come back to——' she hesitated '—because of legal things. Evidence and so on, so he'll be able to tell me how you are.'

Steve, that nice teddy-bear of a man, pressed her hand hard. 'I'll be seeing you,' he said. 'Look after yourself.'

The taxi snorted away and they were gone.

Carefully, concentrating on what she was doing, Lucie packed up her belongings and carried them to the villa next door. She set her travelling bag just inside the big living-room. She wouldn't unpack, because she didn't know where she would be sleeping tonight. If she agreed to Guy Devereux's cynical bargain would he expect——? *No!* she wouldn't let herself dwell on that. The idea of him as a lover sent waves of something like terror coursing through her body.

Instead she would think of her father. She looked round the big, luxurious, impersonal room that had been his home. Had she ever really known him? Which was the real man—the glamorous, overwhelming father of her childhood, always with a big hug for her and a fabulous new doll? Or the angry, dictatorial bully she had fled from in Paris? Or the father she had found here when she came back to him—quieter, more subdued, more affectionate? Had he admitted to himself, she wondered, that he had finally failed, that he was—as Guy had said—on the verge of bankruptcy? No, not the great Warren Martin, not the shrewd, thrusting, resourceful man of business who moved millions of pounds about without turning a hair. He would never admit he was beaten, he would fight to the last ditch.

Now he couldn't fight any longer. It was sad and somehow pathetic, as it inevitably was when a man who had always been a winner had, at last, to suffer defeat. But how comforting it was that he had sent for her, had wanted to make up their quarrel, had shown real affection for her. She was so very, very glad that she had decided to come.

But now he had gone, and others had to deal with the wreck of his empire. Others would have to suffer, through no fault of their own. And that included James—unless—unless——

Oh God, she thought, covering her face with her hands, what am I going to do? All night long her mind had churned backwards and forwards; her father's horrible death, Guy Devereux's revelation, the threat to James's company, to his whole future. And never for an instant had she been able to push away the question that loomed, huge and inescapable over everything else. Would she—*could* she bring herself to marry Guy Devereux for the sake of saving James's company? Surely, she argued, it wouldn't be the end of the world for him. Surely he could start again somehow, he was still young enough, only in his late thirties.

She walked out on to the verandah and stood leaning on the wooden rail. The white strip of beach was almost deserted at this hour, except for a group of early-morning swimmers. There was no breeze and the leaves of the coconut palms hung motionless. The blue expanse of water looked serene and peaceful. Yet it could be cruel, too. Lucie bit her lip, turning her back on the fabulous view, and as she did so she heard the sound of a car approaching.

She spun round. Yes, it was Guy, pulling up the car with a spatter of sand. He got out and came towards her with his long, loping stride and her insides tightened as she waited for him.

He didn't waste time on greetings. 'Your brother just phoned,' he told her. 'He's on his way.'

'Oh!' Lucie let out a long sigh of relief and sank into a chair. 'Oh, that's marvellous, when will he arrive?' For the first time in many hours the world seemed to be straightening itself on its axis.

Guy leaned back against the rail and looked down at her as if he hadn't heard her question. Then he jerked his head back. 'Arrive? Oh, it's uncertain. Depends on how he can link up flights. But Europe is five hours ahead of us, so it's just possible he might get here much later today. Possible, but not likely.'

'Tomorrow, then?' she asked eagerly.

'Oh yes, certainly tomorrow.'

Lucie twisted her fingers together. 'What did he say—what did you tell him?'

'He was worried about you, and how you were coping. I reassured him on that point. I told him I was looking after you.'

'You know James? You've met him?'

Guy shook his head. 'No. I doubt if your father took his managers into his confidence about his financial dealings. I explained my credentials briefly, that was all.'

'So James doesn't know about the—about the situation?'

'Not from me, he doesn't.'

She glanced up uncertainly at him. He was even more curt and indifferent than usual this morning. Why on earth would a man like him want to marry her—her particularly? she wondered again. If he merely wanted a wife there must be dozens—hundreds of girls who would suit him better than she would. Girls who would be impressed by his position and wealth, who would fit gladly into his life-style, who wouldn't object to having a dominating husband—for the sake of the glamour he would provide. Girls who were different in every way from her.

He might have followed her thoughts. He said, 'Well, have you decided to make the great sacrifice?'

She braced herself to be as cool and impersonal as he was. 'I've been considering it, but I need to see my brother first before I give you my answer.'

The dark eyebrows rose. 'I imagined you would want to be in a position to reassure him.'

'I need to see him first,' she repeated stubbornly. 'Getting married may be merely a useful step for you from a business point of view, but I don't look upon it that way. I hate big business—and money—and everything that goes with it. So really I shouldn't be much use to you as a wife.' She spoke more emotionally than she had intended.

The dark-blue magnetic eyes settled on her flushed cheeks. 'You might leave me to be the best judge of that,' he said, and in spite of herself she felt a disturbance deep inside her. She was no seventeen-year-old now to be frightened by a sexual challenge, she assured herself. And she had to face the fact that Guy was a very sexy individual. But sex without love——?

She heard herself say guardedly, 'If I agreed woul‹ you undertake to release me after the two-year perio‹ if I asked you?'

Again that faint, tantalising smile. 'If I couldn' manage to satisfy you in two years then I shoul‹ consider that I'd failed. And I don't include the wor‹ failure in my vocabulary.'

She met his eyes resolutely. '*Would* you promise?' she repeated.

For a moment he seemed to hesitate. Then he said curtly, 'Yes.'

For a long moment they glared at each other lik‹ two fencers. Then he straightened up. 'I must go, have work to do. I'll leave you here to wait for you‹ brother.' He turned without another word and drov‹ away without a backward look.

Lucie sat stiffly where he had left her. Now sh‹ was really on her own. Now there wasn't even Jame‹ to turn to, because she couldn't tell him the truth. Sh‹ must make what should be the most importan‹ decision of her life with no one to help her.

Blossom arrived and fussed over her kindly making her coffee, insisting that she ate som‹ breakfast.

'I will come back this evening and cook for you, she promised before she left. 'My brother catche‹ plenty of turtles. I will make you turtle stew—ver‹ good.' She rolled her beautiful dark eyes.

Lucie hadn't the heart to refuse, and indeed sh‹ was glad to talk to the pleasant black girl. She tol‹ Lucie about her family—her parents had moved t‹ the Caymans from Jamaica five years ago, with thei‹ family of three boys and two girls. 'Plenty of job‹

ere,' Blossom grinned widely. 'More visitors come
very year.'

The hours dragged after Blossom left. Lucie
wouldn't go far from the villa in case James
telephoned. Guy might have given him the number
f the villa. If only she could speak to him, even on
the telephone, it would release some of the tension
that was building inside her.

She sat on the verandah in the shade as the sun
rose higher and a heat-haze settled over the water.
When it got too hot for comfort she stripped off and
lay on her bed, hoping to make up some of the sleep
she had missed last night. Then she panicked,
thinking that Guy might come in unannounced and
find her naked. Her heart thudding, she jumped up
and put on a blue beach-dress and prowled restlessly
from the living-room to the verandah. She dared not
venture out on the beach among the sunbathers
because she had no sun-tan lotion, and getting
herself burned would be idiotic. She had enough to
worry about without that.

Somehow the hours passed. Blossom returned
with the promised turtle stew, carried in a covered
basket, and after she had gone Lucie managed to eat
a tablespoonful of it and tipped the rest down the
waste disposal, feeling guilty and ungrateful.

The sky began to show streaks of flame and palest
green as the sun set, out of sight, to the west of the
island. Lucie watched, the exquisite colours filling
her consciousness for a time with pleasure, and then,
suddenly, it was dark.

She closed the windows against the insects, then
turned on the TV and watched an American film

without having any idea what it was about. Oh,
only something would happen! If only she weren
alone! Even Guy Devereux's unwelcome presenc
would be better than this eerie feeling of utte
solitude. She closed her eyes and tears trickle
behind her lids and down her cheeks.

A knocking sound had her on her feet and rushin
to the door.

James stood there, big and dear and blessedl
familiar, and she threw herself into his arm:
jabbering incoherently. He held her tightly as the
went into the living-room, arms round each other

'Poor little Lucie, what a time you must have had
I got here as soon as I could.'

'Oh, Jimmy—oh, I'm so *glad* you're here! I can
tell you——' she gulped, and pressed her head for
moment against his strong shoulder. Then, with a
effort, she pulled herself together. She must kee
control—keep her wits about her, not give way t
self-pity.

She settled James on a sofa and poured him a glas
of his favourite Scotch and sat beside him. 'Whe
did you get here? I didn't dare hope you might mak
it today.'

'I didn't think I could, I've been unbelievabl
lucky with flights.' He glanced at his watch. 'Afte
we landed I went straight to the address th
Birmingham office gave me—it turned out to be th
hotel where this bloke Devereux is staying, so I wa
able to see him and find out where you were and—
other things. He didn't want to tell me at first, but
could see from his manner that something was ver
wrong, something I didn't know about, and I presse

im. I couldn't understand at first why Father's
ankers were so involved in all this, but in the end he
ame out with it.' He was silent for a moment and
en said heavily, 'It seems that Father was wiped
ut—broke.'

Lucie nodded. 'I know.'

They stared at each other in silence. Then James
aid, 'It's bad, Lucie. It's very bad, little girl.' He
oked away from her.

'For you?' she said, very low.

He turned his head and she was shocked by the
xhaustion and desperation she saw there. James
ad always been optimistic, reassuring, but now he
oked—beaten.

'For all of us,' he said heavily. 'All Father's
ompanies are involved.'

'Couldn't you—couldn't you somehow save the
ompany—make a—what do they call it?—a co-
perative, or something?' Lucie urged.

He shook his head slowly. 'Not a hope. We've
een running dry of capital for some time. You can't
eep a business going if you're coming up against a
ash-flow shortage all the time. One or two bad debts
an tip it over the edge. I've been working like stink
or months filling the order book. I hoped to make
'ather see reason about putting more capital into the
ompany. And now——' He spread out his hands
opelessly.

'I see,' Lucie said in a small voice. She didn't really
nderstand the business jargon, but she could see it
as as bad as it could be.

But a short time later she knew that she was
histaken. It was even worse.

'I think I'll try to contact Angela,' James sai
abruptly, going over to the phone. As he started t
dial Lucie stood up and went out to the kitchen an
put the coffee percolator on. There was something i
her brother's expression that told her that this coul
be a very private conversation.

She closed the door. If he got through to Angel
she would hear him talking, but not what he saic
But there wasn't a sound from the next room. Sh
waited for what seemed ages and was probably abou
ten minutes and then she went back into the living
room.

James was sitting slumped in a corner of the sofa
He shook his head as she asked, 'No reply? But won
she be in bed now? It must be early in the morning i
England.'

'The phone's by the bed,' said James. 'She's nc
there.'

'Not——' Lucie's voice faltered. 'You mean——'

'I mean Angela's left me,' he said, and for
moment Lucie thought he was going to cry.

She went and sat on the sofa by him and took hi
cold hand in hers. So often James had given he
comfort, now she must try to help him. She didn't as
any questions, but after a time James began to talk
in an odd expressionless voice, as if he were thinkin
aloud.

'It's the old story, I suppose I've seen it coming fo
some time. I've hardly been at home except to fa
into bed, exhausted, for weeks. Wives won't tak
that these days, you can't expect them to.'

Couldn't you? Lucie thought. That wasn't her ide
of marriage. Couldn't you expect a wife to under

stand and support her husband when he was in difficulties? She felt a violent surge of anger towards the pretty, self-centred Angela whom James loved. He was too good for her, too understanding, she thought almost bitterly. But he loved her, and that was that.

'It came to a head when I had to leave for this last trip. It was our wedding anniversary later that week and I'd forgotten about it.' He sighed deeply. 'She said, "If you go, I shan't be here when you come back." She's threatened to leave before—this time it seems she's done it.'

'But—but where would she go—and what about the girls?'

'To her mother's, I suppose.' James's voice was infinitely weary. 'And the girls would go there at the weekend. I'd hoped—if this European trip went well—to persuade Father to back the company. If I could have had the funds to take on another couple of men in the department I could have taken it a bit more easily—been home more—you know. Given Angela a better life.'

'But now—with all this happening——' He shook his head and half smiled as his eyes met Lucie's, and she thought she had never seen anything as moving as that half-smile. 'It's the end of the road, Lucie,' he said. 'For Martin's Containers—and for me.' His head drooped and he stared wretchedly at his hands.

Lucie drew in a short breath. 'James——'

Something he heard in her voice made him lift his head. 'Yes?'

'Didn't Guy Devereux say anything to you about—any plans he might have for your company?

About the possibility of saving it?'

'No.' He looked blank.

'I think there might be a chance,' she said. 'He told me yesterday that as it was going to be a—a family matter your company might get special consideration.'

James frowned. 'What on earth does that mean, Lucie?'

'This is going to be a surprise to you, Jimmy, it's been a surprise to me. But that's how these things happen sometimes.'

She threw back her head as she smiled at him. 'Jimmy, wish me joy. Guy and I are going to be married. He'll be your brother-in-law.'

CHAPTER FIVE

'MARRIED?' James's wide brow creased into a frown of amazement; he gaped at her, stunned. 'This isn't a joke, Lucie?'

She shook her head, willing herself to smile happily.

'But you've only known the man a couple of days—how can you——?'

'Oh no, Jimmy, we've known each other much longer than that. We met in Paris, years ago. And then when we saw each other again here it was——' she shrugged '—just one of those things. You know how it is.'

'Yes, I know how it is,' he said, and she thought she heard an unusual touch of cynicism in his voice.

'Probably it wouldn't have happened so quickly if it hadn't been for—for the accident. But Guy's been so marvellous—he's looked after me and done everything that had to be done, and last night we had dinner together and we decided that there was no point in waiting.'

James nodded. 'I see.'

'Aren't you going to say you're glad? Oh, Jimmy dear, please say you're glad!' Lucie put a hand on his arm, pleading with him. 'I know it's been a shock, but I really am very happy.' She *must* convince him. It would spoil everything if he guessed the truth.

He squeezed her hand, then he leaned over and kissed her. 'If it's what you want, of course I'm glad, little sister.' He used the old pet name of her childhood. 'It's just that——' he paused, weighing his words. 'I expect Devereux's a very good man and he can give you all the material things in life. But somehow, I shouldn't have thought——' He broke off again. 'What about Peter? What happened to him?'

Lucie pulled a face. 'Oh, Peter. That's over, it was never anything very much. He came out here with me and he wanted us to be engaged, but it wouldn't have worked. He left after the party.'

'That was very sudden, wasn't it?'

She said, 'He saw how it was with Guy and me.' But had that been the real reason? For the first time since she had read Peter's letter yesterday morning she wondered exactly why he had disappeared so suddenly. He and Guy had talked that night, at the hotel. Had Guy disclosed that Warren Martin's financial empire was in ruins, that there would be no rich inheritance for his daughter? Was money the reason why Peter had suggested coming here with her—had proposed marriage—had said he loved her? Because he had just found out that she had a millionaire father living in the Cayman Islands?

There was a silence. James's thoughts had evidently taken a different turn, because he said, a little awkwardly, 'How was it with Father, Lucie? Was it difficult for you, meeting him again?'

She nodded sadly. 'A bit, at first. But—oh, Jimmy, I'm so glad I came. We—sort of—made up our quarrel and he was so sweet to me, you wouldn't believe. He didn't seem like the same man.' She blinked away quick tears. 'It's so awful that he had to go like that—I'm sure if he'd lived he would have managed to get out of this financial mess he seems to have left behind.'

'I wonder,' James said slowly, and they were both silent again.

Then Lucie summoned up an encouraging smile from somewhere and said, 'But it's going to be all right for you, Jimmy, I know it is. You and Guy must get together and make plans.' She added rather timidly, 'And Angela will come round, I'm sure she will. She really loves you, Jimmy—I expect she just got bored with her own company, with the girls away at school.'

James patted her hand. 'I expect it'll work out somehow,' he said wearily. 'We'll just have to wait and see, won't we?' Then he cheered up with an obvious effort. 'Anyway, something good seems to have come out of all this mess, Lucie, if you're going to be happy. You are, aren't you?' he added, watching her face carefully.

'I'm going to be blissfully happy,' she said. 'Guy's the most wonderful thing that ever happened to me.'

They both turned as there was a slight movement from the direction of the doorway. Guy Devereux stood there, smiling broadly. He looked as if he had been there for some time. 'Right on cue to hear what a lover likes to hear!' He came into the room. 'Forgive me for walking in unannounced—the door was open.' He put his arm round Lucie. 'How are you, darling?'

'Fine,' she said automatically. 'I'm fine.' He was going to kiss her, and she panicked. His head came down and as his mouth touched hers she drew away instinctively, but the pressure of his lips told her everything he wasn't saying: that she was his possession now—he made the rules and she obeyed. He kept his mouth against hers until, with a tiny sigh, she relaxed and her lips softened and responded to his. And in that split second her heart seemed to miss a beat and then start to race, and she knew that she wanted him to go on kissing her.

He released her but kept an arm round her waist. 'You've broken the glad news to your brother, darling. I hope he's not too stunned.' He turned to James. 'I'd have told you earlier, but I thought Lucie would like to tell you herself. I'm afraid we've rushed things rather, but the circumstances have been somewhat traumatic, as you can imagine.'

The two men looked at each other in silence for a moment. Then Guy said, 'I promise to look after her, James.'

James's broad face suddenly broke into a smile. 'You'd damn well better, or I'll probably knock your head off!' He held out a large hand. 'Congratulations,' he said. 'You've got yourself a grand girl.'

'I know it.' Guy took the hand that was offered.

He was a good actor, Lucie thought with contempt, and her mind went back to the times she had watched her father manipulating his business associates. Putting on the charm when there was something he wanted. Guy was working on James now in just the same way, and she could see the charm beginning to take effect. She had a crazy wish to warn him, to yell, 'Don't believe a word of it, Jimmy, he's just getting you on his side because he thinks you might be useful to him. Because he knows you mean a lot to me. Because for some reason he thinks he wants to marry me—probably because he thinks I'm young enough for him to mould into the kind of wife he wants. Nothing to do with love, of course.'

She sank into a chair, her head spinning. What was she thinking of? How could she possibly warn James against Guy, the man who was going to save James's company—possibly also his marriage? For the first time, she was going to have to deceive James, to lie to him. And even though it was in his own interest, it hurt to have to do it. She put a hand to her lips, which were still burning after Guy's almost brutal assault on them. If he could kiss her like that here, in her brother's presence, how would he behave when he got her alone in a bedroom? She remembered the night in the Paris garden and felt a shudder pass through her.

'Don't you think so, Lucie?'

'Mm?' She tried to drag her attention back to what Guy had just said. 'Sorry, I'm afraid——'

'Poor little girl, you're fagged out.' Guy drew her against him and rubbed his cheek gently against her hair. 'We won't talk any more tonight, James. Perhaps you'll come to my office in the morning and we can make provisional plans to tide us over the next few weeks.' He glanced around the room. 'Will you be OK here for tonight? I expect you'll appreciate a good sleep to get over the journey and the jet-lag. I'll take Lucie along with me and look after her, if that's all right with you.'

He didn't wait for James to reply. He picked up Lucie's travelling bag, which was still sitting beside the door, where she had left it. 'Come along, darling.' He held out a hand to her.

Oh no, you don't, Lucie thought. I'm not your slave yet, Mr Guy Devereux. You can wait until we're married before you start giving orders! She smiled sweetly at him. 'Sorry, darling, I can't leave yet. I want to get James a meal first. He can have the bedroom I had when I arrived, but I must put clean sheets on the bed and——'

It was James who interrupted. 'Lucie love, don't fuss, there's a good girl. I couldn't eat a thing, all I want is somewhere to lie down and sleep, and I couldn't care less about sheets—or no sheets, for that matter.' He tried to grin, but it was a poor effort and she saw that he did, indeed, look tired to death.

'Well, if you're sure——' She still hovered uneasily. Where did Guy intend to take her, and what would he want of her?

'I'm quite sure,' James almost groaned, and it was plain that he couldn't wait for her to go. 'Good night, Lucie, see you in the morning.'

She kissed him. 'Good night, Jimmy dear, there's food in the kitchen if you want anything, and the maid will be here in the morning and——'

Guy took her arm and urged her out of the room.

'You heard what the man said, don't fuss, there's a good girl.' He was laughing at her as he led her out of the room and almost pushed her into his car. He slung her bag on the back seat and drove away with a roar of the powerful engine. It sounded to Lucie like a flourish of triumph.

She sat stiffly on the passenger seat. 'Where are you taking me? To your hotel?'

The car reached the road and swung out to the left, away from Georgetown and the hotel. 'No, I've checked out there. We're going to a condo, further along Seven Mile Beach—belongs to a friend of mine, Derek Hatt, who isn't using it just now.'

'Oh.' Lucie kept her eyes straight in front of her. The hood of the convertible was down and the cool breeze blew through her hair, flicking it over her eyes. The headlights shone whitely on the lush greenery along the road and the sky above was dark and moonless. A beautiful night, a beautiful place, a place to be enjoyed, and here she was—unhappy and guilty and darkly apprehensive about the turn that her life had taken. She stole a glance at the man beside her, and was disturbingly conscious of the hard body inside the light jacket. Oh God, she groaned inwardly, what have I let myself in for?

'Wait in the car for a few minutes,' Guy instructed her when the car arrived at its destination. 'I have to pick up the key from the next-door apartment.'

Lucie looked at the spread of low buildings dotted about among the palm-trees. Lights glowed from the windows, illuminating lawns, swimming-pool, balconies. One condo in Grand Cayman was much the same as another, she remembered. All expensive, luxurious, made for people with a life-style that she had rejected. A life-style that, it seemed, she was going to have to accept again—for a time at least. And the shorter the time the better. But what was two years, she tried to persuade herself, out of a whole life? James had done so much for her, surely she could do this for him without grouching.

Guy's tall form loomed out of the shadows. 'Derek said on the phone that they'd left here only last week,' he said, putting the key in the lock, 'so things should be in reasonable order.'

He switched on all the lights and went back to the car for Lucie's bag and his own. Then he made another journey and returned bearing two large bulging carrier bags. 'I took the precaution of laying in some provisions for us.'

Lucie followed him into the immaculate kitchen— all silver-grey and chromium—and watched while he unloaded his purchases. Bread, butter, exotic salads in white plastic containers, more containers with made-up delicacies, a colourful selection of fruit and two bottles of wine. 'This should do us for tonight,' he said. 'Are you hungry? I am.'

'Not very,' she said distantly. 'The maid brought me some turtle stew, earlier this evening. It was delicious.' She didn't tell him that she had thrown most of it away.

'Oh well, you can watch me eat,' Guy said cheerfully. 'I rather fancy one of these pizzas. Stick one in the microwave, will you, Lucie, while I make some coffee.'

She looked at the intimidating appliance on the worktop and the battery of coloured touch-pads seemed to leer back at her. 'I can't use one of these things,' she said.

'Not use a microwave? A fine wife you're going to make!' He was laughing at her.

She tilted her chin. 'Perhaps you'd like to change your mind, then?'

He stripped the packing film from the pizza. 'I think not,' he said. 'I don't choose a wife on the grounds of her cooking ability. I have other activities in mind for you, my girl.'

The vibrant blue eyes passed over her, seeming to strip her of her cotton dress, and she felt the heat rising to her cheeks. For a long moment their glances met and held, and it was as if she were going down in a lift.

Then, abruptly, Guy pushed the pizza in the little oven, closed the door and manipulated the touch-pads. 'Look,' he said, 'I'll show you how this works. It's one of the latest—trust old Derek for that, he's a push-over for technology. Now, this is the mode you use when you want to cook or heat pastry. You touch this pad——'

Lucie wasn't listening. She was acutely aware of him, standing close beside her to demonstrate. As he leaned towards the microwave oven she could feel his breath on her cheek, smell the cologne he used on his thick, smooth hair. His arm, in its thin shirt, brushed against her bare arm, sending tremors shooting through her. She felt weak and breathless as the man's sexual magnetism tugged at her.

'You see how it works?' He turned his head and she stared back at him with glazed eyes.

His own eyes dilated slightly. 'Lucie?' The dark brows went up.

She couldn't speak or move. When his arms went round her and his mouth touched hers she was lost in a new world of sensation. She closed her eyes and her lips parted to his, then a slow burning started low down and began to spread over her body as his hands moved downwards from her waist, drawing her against him. Thrill after thrill rippled through her, leaving her limbs weak and shaking. These were the sensations she had half glimpsed that night in the garden in Paris, but she had been so young, so inexperienced then, and her own rush of desire had terrified her.

'Oh God, Lucie——' Guy's voice came brokenly as he buried his mouth in the hollow of her neck and for a moment they stood locked together as he held her tightly against him as if he were staunching a wound.

Then, abruptly, he released her and turned away. Lucie had to hang on to the edge of the worktop to steady herself. She was dazed and quite unable to think; all she wanted was to be back in his arms.

When he looked round at her his face was wry. 'That wasn't on the agenda,' he said. 'Not at this stage of the proceedings. And there isn't any rose-bed for you to push me into here, so I was taking an unfair advantage.'

Five bleeps came from the microwave oven and Guy opened the door and took out the pizza. 'I've no intention of apologising for a perfectly normal little incident,' he said, and it occurred to Lucie that he was probably mistaking her stunned silence for angry resentment. 'Anyway, I'm hungry.'

He found cutlery and set a knife and fork on the breakfast bar, opened a pack of butter and sliced a crusty loaf. Then, without further ado, he sat down and began to eat.

Lucie stood transfixed, feeling like a zombie, mindless and will-less. A perfectly normal little incident, he had said. Well, it probably was—for him. For the first time she wished she had taken time off from her resolute dedication to her art to learn more about men and what to expect from them. She was painfully at a loss with a man like Guy Devereux.

She searched desperately for something to say and her eyes went to the pizza, adorned with mushrooms and colourful bits of this and that, which was fast disappearing. 'I think I'm hungry after all,' she said in a very small voice.

Guy looked up with a grin and waved his fork towards the packet of pizzas. 'Help yourself. Pop one on the oven tray and time it five minutes on high speed.'

Twenty minutes later they were sitting in the living-room of the apartment with a tray of coffee between them on a low table.

'I feel much more like a human being now.' Guy leaned back in a big, cushiony chair, and stretched his long legs out in front of him. 'It's been quite a day, one way and another. But the ending of the day makes up for the rest of it.'

Lucie sipped her coffee and said nothing. Indeed, she had hardly spoken since that shattering moment when she had found herself in Guy's arms.

'I mean,' he said, 'that it's good to have crossed one hurdle.'

'Hurdle?' she murmured.

He smiled, that narrowed, piercing blue smile. 'Don't pretend you don't know what I'm talking about. I mean you've finally had to admit to yourself that you're not exactly immune to my—er—alluring charms.'

'Have I?' she said woodenly. So she had been wrong, he *had* known what was happening to her, damn him. He *had* known how much she wanted to relax and respond to his kisses.

'My sweet, I wish you'd get out of the habit of batting questions back at me like ping-pong balls. It doesn't make for interesting conversation.'

'I don't particularly want to converse with you.'

'No? Well, I want to be able to converse with you. You're an intelligent girl, and I'm not the kind of man who expects to live *quite* all his married life in bed, you know.' There was a certain sharpness in his tone.

Lucie winced painfully. Oh God, why had she given him a chance of humuliating her like this? Why couldn't she have smacked his face as she had done that night in Paris? But what would have been the good of that, she thought, she was going to marry him. Of her own free will she had laid herself open to any taunt he cared to throw at her. Which wasn't to

 y that she couldn't fight back. She would have to
ather all her strength and her wits together,
herwise he would walk all over her, as her father
ad done.

'I'm glad to hear that,' she said stiffly. 'I've never
elieved that marriage begins and ends in bed.'

'I'd like ours to begin there, anyway.' Guy poured
mself a whisky from a decanter he had found in a
inks cupboard. 'And talking of our marriage, I
ant it to take place as soon as possible. I expect
our brother will have to get back to England soon
ter the funeral, but it would be nice if he could stay
ng enough to see us married. I don't imagine
ere'll be much difficulty in getting a licence, I'm
etty well known around these parts. I'll get in
uch with the official concerned tomorrow.'

Lucie glared at him. 'Haven't you forgotten
mething? I don't remember you asking me what *I*
anted. As a matter of fact I would prefer to wait
ntil we get back to England.'

'You fancy a white church wedding with all the
immings?' he mocked.

'Certainly not. If I took marriage vows in church it
ould be because I loved my husband and intended
keep those vows. In the circumstances I would
gree only to a civil wedding. But I won't be rushed
to it.'

'Won't?' he said gently, raising his eyebrows.
Don't forget you're not exactly in a position to
ctate terms, my love. What I say goes, and I say
e're going to be married as soon as possible. I shall
ave to stay in the Caymans for a while; there's a lot

of work to be got through here, your father's companies are all registered here and the bank's lawyer will be coming out presently. It will be more convenient if you're my wife.'

Suddenly Lucie's mind became very clear. She saw that until this minute she had acted on impulse. Her first need had been to save James from what seemed to be a break-up of his whole life. Now she was beginning to appreciate fully what she was letting herself in for if she married Guy Devereux.

He was arrogant, hard, domineering, high-handed, and his life was devoted to the soulless task of manipulating money. In short, he was everything that she disliked most in a man. She had to admit, after what had just happened in the kitchen, that he disturbed her physically, but that made it even worse, would put her even more in his power.

Guy put down his glass and sauntered across the room. Out of the corner of her eye she saw him leaning nonchalantly against the window-frame, arms folded, watching her. This was a trial of strength between them and would set the pattern for their future relationship—if there was going to be one.

It's not too late, she thought, I could tell him I'd decided not to go through with it. I never promised to marry him. He took it for granted because of what he overheard me saying to James. I could refuse his blackmail even now. Perhaps (a small, tempting voice murmured) it would even be wrong to interfere with James's life. Perhaps she should let him take his own knocks. But—bankruptcy? And his marriage

nd the little girls? And the prospect of the Martin
ame being splashed all over the sensational dailies?

'Well?' The intense blue gaze was fixed on her
lentlessly.

She lifted her chin a fraction. She said, 'I should
arn you that I shan't be a submissive wife, if that's
hat you're expecting. I will keep the contract in the
tter, but I can't promise to keep it in the spirit. If
ou still want to marry me and will keep your
romise about James's company, then I agree to
arry you when and where you decide.'

'Good,' he said briskly. 'I'm sure we're going to get
a splendidly. And now, if you've finished your
offee, I mustn't keep you from your bed any longer.
Ve'll have a look at the bedroom accommodation,
iall we?'

Lucie's heart began to beat painfully as he led the
ay round the luxury apartment. 'Three bedrooms,'
e said finally. 'That's OK. Derek says we can have
ie place for up to a month—they won't be coming
ack themselves just yet.'

'The small room at the back will do me splendid-
,' she said, wishing she could keep her voice steady.

'Oh, I don't think so.' Guy carried her travelling
ag into the largest room of the three and put it down
a the double bed. 'We can do better than that for
ou. You can lie here and look out at the sea.'

She passed her tongue over her dry lips. 'I don't
ally need a room this size all to myself.'

He stood beside the door regarding her under
iick dark lashes. 'What exactly are you trying to tell
ie?'

That I'm scared stiff, she wanted to say. That t
whole situation terrifies me. She had begun to sha
uncontrollably. 'I—I——' she stammered.

He came across the room and put his hands on h
shoulders, and at his touch she jumped like a startl
rabbit. 'Don't worry, Lucie,' he said quite gent]
'I'm not about to ravish you, if that's what you'
afraid of. You can have the main bedroom all
yourself, until we're married. Then I shall expect
be allowed to share it with you, is that understood

'Yes,' she whispered.

'James can join us here tomorrow, there's plenty
room for all three of us and you'll have an excelle
chaperon,' he added with that touch of irony that s]
had come to expect. 'Now I suggest that you go
bed and get a good night's sleep. I've got a lot
paperwork to get through before I turn in. Goo
night, Lucie.' He touched her cheek briefly and we
out.

Lucie looked at the closed door and felt that s]
had been dismissed. She was relieved that he had le
her alone, of course she was, she assured herself.
was only her feminine pride that made her feel th
odd sense of disappointment.

The days that followed had the feeling of a drea
sometimes events crowding in on each other, ar
then long intervals when Lucie was alone with h
fears and doubts about the future. It was the waitir
that was so nerve-racking, having no idea what tl
future would hold: where she would live, and wh
life-style would be expected of her. All the things :

ngaged couple should be discussing constantly were
 closed book to her. Guy made no attempt to speak
f their future together and Lucie would rather have
ied than ask him.

She bought pencils and paper in Georgetown and
ied to make preliminary sketches for her next
ook, but the urge had gone. Most of the time she sat
n the patio trying to read, or just lay back and let the
eat of the sun soak into her. She couldn't bring
erself to swim in the sea alone, but there was a
esh-water pool in the grounds of the condo
omplex, and she swam there now and again and
nade friends with some of the children staying in the
eighbouring apartments. One or two of her new
eighbours made friendly overtures, but she smiled
nd thanked them and refused their invitations to
in their parties on outings or picnics or for drinks,
nd after a day or two they took the hint and left her
one.

Sometimes James joined her for an hour or two,
ut mercifully she saw very little of Guy. Most of the
nanagers of Warren Martin's companies had ar-
ved, and there were endless meetings at the bank's
fice in Georgetown, usually going on until late in
ne evening. 'To try to sort out the almighty mess,'
ames told her.

When she and Guy were together it was always in
ames's presence; Lucie noticed that when James
ctfully tried to leave them together Guy always
nanaged to outwit him. It was, she thought, almost
s if he didn't want to be alone with her. Perhaps he
as afraid that James would guess the truth but,

whatever the reason, Lucie was relieved of the stra
of being alone with him. And in the wake of th
tragedy she couldn't be expected to behave like
blissful engaged girl when the three of them wer
together, so as the days passed she was sure tha
James suspected nothing unusual in the situation

James himself began to revive as the days passe
'I think we're going to come out of it OK,' he to
Lucie. 'It's been touch and go, but Guy has bee
pretty darned marvellous about it. He's mastermin
ing a huge reorganisation and it looks almost certai
that all Father's companies will be able to carry on i
one way or another.'

No scandal, then? No jobs lost? No scurrilo
headlines in the papers?

'I'm glad,' said Lucie, and that sounded pathet
cally inadequate when she considered what th
alternative might have been.

'You've got yourself a remarkable bloke ther
little sister,' James told her, with more than a touc
of hero-worship. 'A mind like a razor.'

'Yes.' Lucie nodded automatically. A razor tha
would cut through anything that stood between hi
and something he happened to want. A steel blad
keen and cold and sharp.

At the funeral Lucie sat between James and Guy i
the little Anglican chapel and tried not to weep fo
the father she had loved and lost and then foun
again for such a short time. James stared straigh
ahead of him, and she guessed that his feelings wer
quite different from hers. It was Guy who saw tha

she was weeping and his hand covered hers briefly. At that moment Lucie was grateful for the contact, it made him seem a little more human.

Afterwards the few people who had attended the service gathered at the apartment for a buffet lunch. There were Warren Martin's business colleagues and one or two acquaintances that he had made in Grand Cayman; Steve Maddox who had flown from Houston for the inquest and stayed on for the funeral. Giles Blunt, the bank's lawyer, who had arrived only the day before bringing his elegant wife, Cynthia, with him—'for the trip', he had told Lucie when they were introduced.

Giles was a thin, fairish man of about forty with a bony, clever face. He pressed Lucie's hand sympathetically when they were introduced and gave her a nice, friendly smile. Cynthia, on the other hand, subjected her to a hard, assessing glance before she held out a languid hand. She was a striking silver-blonde with a fashionably pencil-thin body and a bored expression. Lucie disliked her on sight; she seemed to represent all the hard, elegant females who had formed part of her father's circle in the bad old days.

The day was turning out stiflingly hot and the air-conditioner could hardly cope with the crowd of bodies in the room. Lucie stood with James and Guy, wearing the blue jersey two-piece suit that she had travelled in. It was much too warm for a day like this, but it had been the only outfit that was remotely suitable for the occasion. She supposed she could have gone out and searched for a black dress, but she couldn't summon up the energy to do it.

The service had been a strain and she felt a headache threatening. She wanted to escape to her room, but these people were, in a way, her guests. Most of the men were gathered round the buffet table. Lucie's glance passed to Cynthia Blunt, who was draped over a sofa looking beautiful and sulky. She was obviously dressed for the occasion, but managed to look sexy at the same time in a very stylish black crêpe-de-chine dress with flowing lace sleeves and a revealing neckline. When she moved a waft of heavy exotic perfume hung on the air all around her. I hope I don't have much to do with her while she's here, Lucie thought fervently.

Steve Maddox came over to their little group to say goodbye, and the three men broke off their conversation while James thanked him sincerely for his help.

Steve took Lucie's hand in his and squeezed it. 'Dorothy sent her love, and you must come and visit with us if you ever come to Houston, Lucie.' He paused, clearing his throat awkwardly. 'It's been a bad time for you, my dear. I hope things go better in the future.'

Guy stepped round James and put his arm possessively across her shoulders. 'They will, I promise you,' he said in a firm voice. 'I'm going to look after her from now on. Lucie and I are getting married next week.'

There was a sudden silence in the room. He had spoken loudly enough to make himself heard to everybody there. Then the congratulations broke out and the men at the buffet table gathered round.

Steve Maddox's plump face broke into a wide grin. 'Gee, now that's quite something to tell Dorothy when I get back! She'll give me no peace till I promise to bring her to the wedding.'

'You'd both be very welcome,' said Guy. 'If you leave your phone number——'

Lucie stood beside him, a small fixed smile on her mouth. How insensitive of him to pick just this moment to make his announcement! Her glance fell on Cynthia Blunt. The bored look had left her face, her cheeks were drained of colour, her eyes narrowed almost viciously. She looked momentarily like someone who had had a very nasty shock and was taking it badly. Then the expression was wiped off her face and replaced by a sweet smile. She rose gracefully. 'Well, this is a bombshell! You should have warned us, Guy darling. Did *you* know, Giles?'

'Not a hint.' Her husband eyed her with a faint smile, his thin lips drawn down at the corners.

Cynthia turned to Guy. 'Well, congratulations and all that, both of you. What a pretty little girl you've found yourself, Guy. *So* clever of you! But then you've always been disgustingly clever, haven't you, darling? I warn you, you'll have quite a job living up to him, Lucie.'

Lucie stared back at her. 'I'm sure Guy will give me all the help I need,' she said sweetly, smiling up at him.

'Try and stop me!' He grinned broadly and bent his head and kissed her on the mouth, and all the men laughed delightedly.

Lucie's knees sagged under her. The feel of Guy's

lips made her heart race. Her head was thumping and she felt faint and she wasn't going to be able to stand much more. She was trying to think how she could get away, when Guy leaned down and said softly, 'I think you've had as much as you can stand, Lucie. I'm going to take you to your room.'

Dimly she heard him making her apologies for her and then his arm was strong round her, leading her out of the heat and noise into the blessed cool of her bedroom.

She sank on to the bed, shielding her eyes from the light. Guy drew the curtains and said, 'Aspirins— have you got any anywhere?'

'On the shelf in the shower-room,' she whispered.

He found the tablets and gave her a glass of water. 'These'll soon do the trick.' He put an arm round her and helped her to sit up while she swallowed the tablets. He was being kind, she thought vaguely, and his arm was strong and comforting. She had a foolish wish to snuggle closer, but instead she drew away and laid her head back on the pillow. She mustn't let him believe she was a weak female who normally needed a man to look after her—that would lead directly to his running her life for her, as her father had once tried to do.

It was quite an effort to speak, but she summoned the energy to say, 'Thank you, Guy, now you get back to the others. I'll be quite better soon.'

He still hovered over the bed. 'Sure? You look very pale.'

She managed to smile. 'I'll be all right. I'm tough, you know.'

He was bending over the bed, his face coming nearer and nearer. 'I don't believe a word of that nonsense,' he said, and kissed her very gently on the mouth. 'Now, go to sleep and don't come out again until you feel quite better. I'll get rid of the crowd soon. Oh, and I nearly forgot—you'd better have this now that the announcement has been made.'

He put something down beside her on the bedside table and then the door shut quietly behind him.

Lucie closed her eyes. It was quite extraordinary, but already her headache was better. She pulled herself up in the bed and found that Guy had left a small envelope on the table. Inside the envelope was a velvet padded box with a ring of black coral, surrounded by tiny pearls, on a thin gold band. On the envelope Guy had written, 'I look forward to buying you diamonds later, but perhaps this local ware will do for the moment. G.'

Lucie slipped the ring on her third finger. It fitted perfectly. It was a beautiful ring and she preferred it to diamonds, but Guy wouldn't have known that. Soon they would be married and they knew nothing about each other—nothing at all. But he had been kind to her just now, so perhaps there was a softer side to him. There was a little smile on her lips as she drifted off into sleep.

After that the days resumed the pattern that Lucie had come to expect. In the daytime she was mostly on her own, in the evenings she would eat out at one of the restaurants along the beach with James and Guy. One evening they were joined by Giles Blunt and the exotic Cynthia, who monopolised the conversation and fluttered her long eyelashes at the men (principally, Lucie noticed, at Guy) and told stories that got more and more risqué until finally her husband put his hand over her wineglass and said, 'That's enough, Cynthia, I think it's time we left.' When they had gone James chuckled and said, 'Quite a girl, that one!' For some reason Lucie found herself waiting for Guy's comment, but he merely smiled his enigmatic smile and said nothing.

Would she ever know what he was thinking? Lucie wondered, watching the inscrutable face. Whatever sort of a marriage could she have with a man so detached, so unforthcoming? She shivered inside as she thought that in only a few days she would know.

CHAPTER SIX

FIVE days later Lucie sat between Guy and James in the hired convertible, as Guy drove towards the Grand Cayman airport. In her new oyster-coloured silk suit, which Guy had chosen for her to wear at the wedding, she felt very conscious that she was being squeezed between the two men—in more ways than the obvious one. She eased herself a little towards James and he put a big arm round her and said, 'Well, well, this has been a very strange time. It will take me until I get back home to come to terms with all that's happened. But at least one good thing has come out of it. You two are going to be very happy and I wish you, once again, all the luck in the world.'

Lucie murmured something unintelligible and Guy turned his head to bestow a dazzling blue smile on her, then cursed as an approaching car swerved violently across the road. 'Bloody fools!' he barked. 'Why can't they remember that you drive on the left here?'

There followed a masculine-type discussion about the accident level in Grand Cayman, which lasted until they reached the airport, and gave Lucie a brief respite from the act she had been putting on since the civil wedding two hours ago.

She had gone through the dry little ceremony as if it were all happening to someone else. And after-

wards, at a restaurant lunch where the only guests
beside James, had been Giles and Cynthia Blunt
and the Maddoxes, Steve and Dorothy—who had
flown over from Houston for another short holiday
especially to be at the wedding—she had smiled until
her lips were stiff from the effort of trying to look like
a blissfully happy bride. But once James had left she
need keep up the pretence no longer. That was one
advantage of the fact that they were, it seemed, to
stay on in the Caymans for at least two more weeks.
By the time she saw James again she would somehow
have managed to get a grip on herself.

James's face, when he kissed her goodbye, was the
one happy thing about her wedding-day. Everything
had taken a turn for him and he was the old James—
positive, cheerful, looking towards the future. He
had had a long phone call to Angela, at her mother's
home, and from his expression afterwards Lucie had
guessed that all had gone well.

'It's going to be all right,' he said afterwards to
Lucie. 'We're going to make plans when I get back.'

As he checked in at the airport and the three of
them made for passport control, she could see that he
could hardly wait to get home to Angela. Just at that
moment James's happiness made up for her own
unknown and frightening immediate future.

He shook Guy's hand. 'Thanks for everything,' he
said seriously. 'You've been our fairy godfather, and
I won't forget it. Angela and I will look forward to
seeing you both when you get back to England.'

He hugged Lucie again and went through the
barrier. Lucie watched until his tall, broad figure was

ost in the crowd. He seemed like the one dear, familiar thing in her world, and she wanted to cry.

Guy took her arm and led her out to the car. 'It seems rather an anticlimax,' he said, as he drove back to Georgetown, 'but I'm afraid I must get back to the office for a short time. I've got a spot of paperwork to finish. What would you like to do? Hang around in the town and wait for me, or I could get a taxi to take you back to the condo?'

'I'll hang around for a while,' she said coolly. She wasn't quite sure what she had expected when they were alone together for the first time since the wedding. But this unconcerned, almost indifferent approach seemed like a slap in the face. 'I have a few things I want to buy, then I'll find a taxi for myself.'

'Just as you like.' He parked the car outside the modern white building where his bank had their office. 'I'll see you later, then.' They might have been married for years, Lucie thought, as she made her way to the waterfront and strolled along by the little harbour, stopping to watch a boat being unloaded at the quayside, a pint-sized crane waving about busily to the accompaniment of much good-humoured shouting and clanking of chains. Georgetown was such a happy place, she thought, everyone seemed to be enjoying themselves—even if they were working. She wondered how long it would be before she felt happy again herself.

In the Viking Gallery she gazed at the beautiful things displayed in the windows—precious gems, porcelain figurines, black and pink coral jewellery,

glittering crystal—she reminded herself that as Gu
Devereux's wife she could afford to buy anythin
that took her fancy, as she had done when she ha
lived with an indulgent father. She smiled sadly t
herself as she remembered how generous that fathe
had been once—how loving and proud of his prett
daughter. And it could have been like that again
only—if only—— She missed him terribly now an
grieved for the loving understanding that hadn't ha
time to mature.

Blinking away the tears, she turned away from th
window. If this had been an ordinary marriage sh
would have gone into the Gallery to buy some lovin
reminder for her husband, but Guy wouldn
appreciate a sentimental gesture of that kind, she fe
sure. Diamond cuff-links would be more in his lin
she thought cynically.

Then she drew back with a little gasp as she sa
Guy himself, strolling along beside the harbour, h
dark head bent towards his companion in earnes
conversation. She was pressing close to him, her arr
linked through his, her white-gold head shining lik
silver in the sunshine, her exquisite face raised to hi
her red-glossed lips parted in a secret little smil
Cynthia Blunt!

Lucie stood like a statue, watching them until the
disappeared round the corner by the camera shop
their heads intimately close. So this was the 'spot c
paperwork' that he had to get through! The empt
feeling inside her wasn't jealousy—it couldn't be
What did it matter to her how many women Guy ha
in his life? She would probably have to turn a blin

ye to many things that went on in this farce of a
marriage. She twisted the new, shining gold ring on
her finger. She was Guy Devereux's wife, heaven
help her, and too much depended on her now for her
to try to back out. Maybe when Guy discovered her
inexperience he would decide to leave her alone.
That was the best thing she could hope for.
Meanwhile, there was her wedding night to be faced.
Her heart sinking, she made her way slowly back to
the taxi-rank beside the harbour.

Guy breezed into the apartment half an hour after
Lucie got back there herself. He looked very pleased
with life.

'Pack a bag, my sweet child, we're off on our
honeymoon!' He grabbed her by the waist and
swung her off her feet.

This was a Guy she hadn't seen before. Perhaps
his meeting with Cynthia Blunt had gone satisfac-
torily. Had he reassured her about the need for him
to have a wife? She could almost hear him saying, 'It
won't make any difference to us, my love.'

She waited until he released her and then
straightened the jacket of her silk suit with care. 'I
shouldn't have thought a honeymoon was necessary,'
she said.

'Necessary? What sort of a word is that? Every
proper marriage must have a honeymoon, even if it's
only three or four days—which is all ours must be, I
fear. A very short honeymoon, but we'll make the
most of it.' He stripped off the light jacket he had
worn for the wedding ceremony and threw it over the
back of a chair. Then he poured himself a long drink

and dropped ice cubes in it. 'You?'

Lucie shook her head and he went on enthusiast
cally, 'We're going to Little Cayman—you know i
The tinier of the two sister islands, and my favourit
place. We can catch a flight to the Brac at a quarte
to four. Allowing for a link-up, we get to Littl
Cayman at five o'clock.'

'I still don't think a honeymoon is necessary—n
with a marriage like this one.' She couldn't brin
herself to say 'a marriage like ours'. That would seen
to join them together, and she needed to keep herse
apart, her own person, not his possession.

She had got his full attention now. 'Well, *I* thin
it's very necessary,' he said, eyeing her thoughtfully
'You're all tensed up, Lucie, you need a break, afte
all that's happened. We both do. We need to rela
Come on now, pack your things—you won't nee
much, only the minimum of covering for day and
jacket in case the evenings are cool. I'll get change
and packed myself.' He went into his bedroon
taking his drink with him.

'—there was some doubt up to the last minut
about whether I could be spared.' His voice reache
her through the open doorway. 'That's why I didn
mention it to you until I was sure. But Giles Blur
says he'll carry on on his own for a day or two. He's
good bloke, Giles is, one of my best friends. You'
like him when you have time to get to know him

Lucie walked over and stood in the doorway of hi
bedroom. 'Shall I like his wife, too?' she aske
evenly.

Guy was stuffing things into a travel-bag. Hi

head jerked round and he was frowning. 'Cynthia? Well, Cynthia might not appeal to you all that much. She's something of an acquired taste.'

A taste you've managed to acquire, she thought cynically. In the sophisticated world that Guy Devereux and his kind inhabited your best friend's wife would be fair game. She had personal experience of that world and she knew it wasn't for her. For her, a marriage without loyalty and trust was no marriage at all. All the more reason, she thought, to end this ridiculous marriage with Guy Devereux as quickly as possible. But how?

'Come on, Lucie, get packing or we'll miss our flight.' There was an edge to his voice now. 'Don't start being difficult. We need a little time to be alone and get to know each other. What's wrong with that?'

'Everything,' she snapped. 'I know all I want to know about you. I've already told you that I hate your kind of life.'

'And what is my kind of life? You haven't lived with me—yet—so you must be guessing.'

She was silent, her mouth set in a mutinous line.

He came over to her, where she stood in the doorway, and put his hands on both her shoulders. As if he were taking her prisoner, she thought a little wildly. She tried to wriggle away, but he held her fast.

'Pack it in, Lucie,' he said sharply. 'You've chosen to marry me, so at least give it a try. Without prejudice,' he added. 'Now go and get out of that stylish outfit, you won't need anything like that where we're going.'

He was so close and he seemed to tower above her, large and muscular and threatening. For a long moment they stared into each other's eyes, and the impact of that dazzling deep blue made Lucie's toes curl up inside her sandals. It was she who looked away first. 'I'll go and get packed,' she muttered, and went into her bedroom.

It would have suited Lucie's mood to hate anywhere that Guy chose to take her to, but from the moment that the tiny plane put down on a golf-course-green runway and two egrets spread their wings and flapped up into the cloudless sky, she knew that there was no way she could hate this place.

A rather ancient Land Rover met them. Guy greeted the driver as an old friend. 'Hello, Sam, great to see you again.'

The driver grinned down at them, teeth shining white against his leathery-brown skin. 'Great to see you Mr Devereux. I got your phone message. You goin' out to Mr Hatt's shack? He was here for some fishing a couple of weeks ago.' He glanced at Lucie and then away again, and she had the impression that he was being tactful and wondered briefly if Guy was in the habit of bringing his girl-friends here.

Sam piled their bags in the back and they climbed up into the wide seat beside him, Guy in the middle. 'Yes, I know,' said Guy, settling back and looking around with a sigh of pleasure as they rattled away along the dusty road. 'I'm hoping he left us plenty of

tins. I didn't want to waste time coming over from
the Brac by boat, so we haven't brought any stores
with us. We're only here for a day or two. Meet my
wife, Sam.'

'Glad to know you, Mrs Devereux.' Sam glanced
at her with a wide grin, and she thought he looked
relieved. 'You call on us if you run out of coffee or
eggs.'

'We'll do that, Sam,' Guy said. 'And how's your
wife keeping? And the boys?'

Lucie looked about her as Sam's low voice, with its
vaguely Welsh lilt, droned on. Guy was right, this
island was very different from Grand Cayman. The
road looked as if it had been carved out by hand from
the bushes and low trees that fringed it. There wasn't
another car or another person in sight on the ten
minutes' drive. She wondered where they were
going. Mr Hatt's shack, Sam had said. That sounded
pretty primitive. Guy had certainly planned to get
her to himself, away from the world. She shivered.

When the Land Rover pulled up no building was
visible. Sam and Guy got out and Sam lifted their
bags on to the road verge. Guy held out his arms to
Lucie. 'Come on, jump,' he urged and she stepped
down awkwardly, trying as far as she could to avoid
his outstretched arms. But he grabbed her and gave
her a tight hug, and Sam favoured them with a wide,
understanding grin as he climbed back behind the
wheel, and drove away with a cheery salute.

Guy picked up their bags. 'Welcome to the
honeymoon hotel,' he said, mocking her obvious
surprise. He held back a heavy branch that overhung

the road. 'Old Derek believes in privacy when he's here.'

Behind the branch a narrow earth-track led between densely-growing bushes. 'You need your machete when you come here,' Guy laughed. 'The landscape has a habit of closing in on you.'

Lucie stumbled along. The pebbles hurt her feet through the thin soles of her sandals and the bushes scratched her bare legs as she pushed her way between them. Guy transferred both the bags to one hand and held out the other to her. 'Not much further,' he encouraged. And then, 'Here we are, this is it. Super, isn't it?'

'Shack' was right, Lucie thought, puzzled. She saw a low wooden building, like something out of a Western movie. The bushes grew right up to the steps that led to the door. Trailing plants dipped across the two windows, which were bare of curtains. Was this where Guy had brought her for their 'honeymoon'? It seemed out of character, not at all what she had expected. But not for the world was she going to admit to him that this place seemed far more her kind of place than some sophisticated hotel or dive-club.

'Come on in.' He ran up the steps. 'Derek doesn't ever lock the door—there's no need here. Not that there's anything inside to pinch.'

She followed him inside the cabin. The door opened into a long, almost-bare room. Venetian blinds covered the far windows and it was difficult to see clearly. There seemed to be a table with an oil lamp on it, a couple of chairs, a writing-desk. At one

nd was a kitchen dresser that had a Victorian look
bout it, furnished with various large bottles and
ins. All this she took in vaguely before Guy came
rom behind and closed his arms around her, his
ands covering her breasts under the thin stuff of her
un-dress. His mouth buried itself in her neck, under
ts curtain of dark hair, and she was angrily aware of
he way her stomach tightened at his touch. Why did
er stupid body have to respond like this? Why
ouldn't she be cool and self-assured like—well, like
Cynthia Blunt, for instance? A woman like that
vould know how to handle a man.

'Come and see,' he said. 'This is the big surprise.'
Ie released her and walked across to pull up the
blinds, one by one.

It was like seeing a brilliantly-lit stage when the
house-lights go down. Straight ahead was a strip of
white sand and then—as far as the eye could see to
both sides—blue, dazzling blue sea. Lucie couldn't
restrain a gasp of pleasure.

'Marvellous, don't you think?' Guy drew her out
on to the covered balcony. 'Some day I'll persuade
Derek to sell this place to me, but he won't part with
t yet, the wretch.' He was like a schoolboy showing
some new treasure. 'But for now it's a super spot for
our honeymoon. Come inside and I'll show you the
bedroom.'

The bedroom! Lucie began to tremble. She leaned
on the balcony rail, staring blindly out to the fine,
dark line of the horizon.

'Come along, girl, I'll need your help, the mattress
will have to be blown up. It's one of those air-beds—

very comfortable when you get used to it.'

She drew in a deep breath. This was idiotic, sh
was twenty-two—well, nearly twenty-two—and sh
was behaving like a kid of fourteen. She though
wryly that these days some girls of fourteen knew
more about sex than she did. Bracing herself, sh
followed Guy into the only other room of the cabin
where he pulled a tyre-pump out from a corner an
attached it to a valve in a limp blue mattress.

'You hang on to that end and hold it straight,' h
ordered. 'No, *straight*,' as she picked up one corner o
the mattress with nerveless fingers.

'I'm not a Girl Guide,' she snapped. 'And I don'
take orders!'

He stopped pumping. '*Please*, Lucie, will you hol
the damned thing straight, and stop being childish,
he said with exaggerated patience.

Pursing her lips mutinously, she did as he aske
and a couple of minutes later the job was done an
the blue mattress lay plumply on the floor. Luci
couldn't bring herself to look at it.

Guy dropped down on to it and rolled abou
luxuriously. 'It's very comfy.' He held up a hand i
invitation. 'Come and try.'

'No,' she muttered. She walked out of the roon
and out on to the verandah. She was shaking so muc
that she had to hold on to the rail to steady herself

He came after her, took her by the shoulders an
turned her to face him. 'Lucie, what is this? You
married me, remember? You're not thinking o
cheating on me, are you?' His tone was restrained
but she quailed as she saw the frozen, dangerous loo

n his face. How could she ever have imagined she
could defy him?

She shook her head speechlessly.

He sighed like a man at the end of his tether. 'Oh
well, let it go for now. We'd better go out and watch
he sunset.'

'Oh, *yes*,' Lucie breathed. 'That would be lovely.'
Anything to put off the moment when she would
have to share that bed with him.

'Lovely!' he echoed drily, leading the way down
he steps to the beach.

There wasn't another soul in sight. They walked
along the edge of the tide, not talking, and gradually
Lucie's tension began to relax. The afternoon heat
had gone; the sea was smooth; the sea-birds that
swooped lazily around were silent. The only sounds
came from the cawing of rooks in the distance and
the soft whisper of little waves that creamed at their
feet. As they walked the sun went down in a haze of
silver-grey and the sky before them was streaked
with apricot and pale green.

Lucie drew in a breath of pure pleasure, the artist
in her revelling in the exquisite colours. 'It's
beautiful,' she said breathlessly. Guy didn't reply,
but when his arm closed round her waist, drawing
her close against him, she didn't pull away.

'I promised you a paradise island, didn't I?' he
murmured. 'Or perhaps a Garden of Eden for just
the two of us.'

He stopped and turned her round to face him.
'You're a very beautiful Eve.' His voice was suddenly
husky. His fingers slid into her dark hair, pushing it

away from her face. He gazed down at her steadil
and what she saw in his eyes sent a throb all throug
her body.

'Lucie!' he muttered. And then, 'I don't think
can wait any longer.'

He lifted her in his arms and carried her up t
where the low-growing trees overhung the beach
dense and thick. When he laid her down on the sur
warmed sand and lowered himself beside her
languor came over her and she stared hazily at th
lean brown face above her own. A pulse began t
beat insistently low inside her, and she groaned wit
an urgency that was new and strange and painfull
intense. Hardly knowing what she was doing, sh
reached up and pulled his head down to hers, movin
her lips recklessly against his until their mouth
seemed to fuse together. All her shyness, all he
resistance to him had gone. Her mind wasn'
working; her body's needs had taken over as sh
clung desperately to him, her fingers digging into th
hard muscles of his shoulders.

For a moment he was very still and she had
terrible fear that he was going to reject her. Perhap
she shouldn't have let him know what he was doin
to her. Perhaps she should have waited for him t
make the first move.

'Guy——' she pleaded. 'Oh, Guy—please——'

Then she felt his weight on her and she seemed t
melt into the sand as his hands explored the sof
warmth of her, pushing aside the straps of he
sundress, closing over the swell of her breasts
moulding them until she moaned with pleasure. Sh

hardly knew what he was doing as the last flimsy garments were removed. Then his own shirt and jeans followed and they were together, naked as Adam and Eve in that first mythical story.

She heard the heavy beating of her heart—or was it his, or both?—and every fear she had ever had dissolved in the sheer magic of this moment. His hands stroked and teased, rousing her to a peak of excitement until she cried aloud for fulfilment.

'Don't be afraid, my darling, I'll try not to hurt you,' he whispered thickly, but Lucie felt nothing but a wild rapture as the whole of her body was taken over by a primitive need until she was burning up in the heat of it. Oh God, she had never known it would be like this. Wave upon wave of pleasure shook her as they moved together more and more urgently, until suddenly she cried out as one last great wave of pure physical ecstasy engulfed her. Guy's face was pressed hard into her shoulder and he shuddered violently and moaned her name aloud. She felt his weight relax on her and wrapped her arms round his moist body before he rolled away and lay still beside her.

Slowly they came back to reality. Guy levered himself up on one elbow and looked down at her, but the sub-tropical darkness had almost fallen and she couldn't see whether there was tenderness in his face.

'You must get some clothes on, you'll get cold,' he said matter-of-factly. He reached over and tossed her sundress to her and pulled on his own jeans and sweat-shirt. Lucie sat up, shivering a little, but she couldn't tell whether it was from cold or something

else. Awkwardly she got into her clothes and pulle
the cotton jacket round her.

Guy stood up and pushed aside the overhangin
branches of sea-grape tree that had formed thei
pivate bower. They walked back in silence, arm
round each other, the way they had come, and nov
the sky was black velvet, thick with stars. 'Incred
ible!' Lucie murmured, looking up at them.

Everything was incredible. She supposed tha
soon ordinary life would begin again, but it wouldn'
be the same life as the one that had seemed to sto
back there under the sea-grape trees.

Guy spoke then. 'Lucie——' He paused uncertain
ly. That was incredible too. Guy, who always ha
complete command of himself, seemed for once to b
at a loss for words.

'Mm?' She looked dreamily up at him. Perhaps h
was going to say he loved her. She waited. Oh
please, please let him say he loves me and then i
won't matter about anything else.

He said, 'Not getting cold, are you? We'd bette
get a move on, it gets chilly at night sometimes.' H
quickened his stride and she had to follow him.

The magic spell had broken. Guy had got what h
had wanted for so long. Had he been disappointed
Now that he had had her would he lose interest'
Misery took her by the throat.

'There's one thing I'm going to insist on,' Guy
said, when they got back to the shack. 'This is ou
honeymoon and this little island is about as far from
the intrusions of the outside world as is possible. S
I'm going to insist that we keep it that way. We sha

ive the present moment as if there were no past—
not even any future, just taking every moment as it
happens.'

He looked deep into her eyes with an expression
that answered her questions and made her shudder
with anticipation. 'Beginning now, Lucie,' he said,
very low, leading her into the bedroom.

Their honeymoon lasted three days, three days
literally out of this world, Lucie thought. Her doubts
melted away, the future could look after itself so long
as she had Guy. Never in her life had she known
happiness like this—how crazy she had been to
believe that her art could ever replace the bliss of
loving!

The days were filled with sunshine and sand and
sea and the multitude of wild birds, fascinating fish,
sea-shells. Guy hired a boat and they took a picnic to
Owen Island, a tiny uninhabited cay paradise just off
the coast.

They swam in the warm shallow sea near the shore
where the water was crystal-clear and the tiny fish
darted about like streaks of coloured light. They
drowsed lazily on the soft pinkish-white sand where
the only sounds were of the dried leaves of the sea-
grapes rustling in the soft breeze, and the buzzing of
bees, and now and again the plopping of a large fish
offshore.

They wandered up the sandy trails from the beach
which led to nothing but the wildness of nature. One
evening they walked along the beach to a landlocked
lake teeming with tarpon—huge silvery glistening
fish that rose so thick when the light was failing that

the lake looked almost solid with them.

One evening they tidied themselves up and dine
at the Southern Cross Club, where Guy seemed t
know almost all the staff and some of the visitors, bu
most of the time they were delightfully alone.

And all the time they revelled more and more i
each other's bodies. Guy's expert, sensitive lovemak
ing was rapture such as Lucie had never imagined
The touch of his hands on her—when they swam i
the warm sea or lay in the shade of the trees, o
turned out the lamp and made love on the air-be
with the moon lighting up the wooden walls and th
big wash-bowl decorated with blue roses—made he
senses shiver with delight. All her shyness forgotten
she learned intuitively, and gloried in her ability t
please him.

'I'm shameless, aren't I?' she challenged him
laughing and winding her ams round his smootl
brown back, twining her legs with his.

'You're adorable, you little witch. I told you, didn'
I,' Guy exulted, 'that we should be good together?

Lucie was deliriously happy, and she tried t
thrust away the one tiny doubt that arose when sh
woke alone in the bed to find that Guy wasn'
there—had gone out for an early swim. Never onc
had he actually said he loved her. She should hav
more faith, she told herself; hadn't he shown, ove
and over again, that he loved her? He just wasn't th
romantic type, that was all, and she mustn't expec
something that he couldn't give.

After four days they went back to Grand Cayman
to Derek Hatt's apartment. As soon as they got back

Guy telephoned to Derek, in New York, to thank him for the loan of the apartment, and the shack in Little Cayman.

'We found it perfect for a honeymoon,' he said casually, with a double-take towards Lucie who was standing beside him; from the explosion at the other end of the line she knew that Guy hadn't told his friend anything about his marriage. 'Yes,' he went on, grinning broadly. 'Last week. Sorry there wasn't time to invite you, chum. Once I managed to get Lucie to agree, I made it legal at the first possible moment. But we must meet up soon with you and Beth. Have a word with my new wife.' He handed the receiver to Lucie.

Derek sounded nice, Lucie thought after a short, friendly conversation, but he couldn't hide his amazement. She replaced the phone and looked up at Guy. 'Obviously he didn't think you were the marrying type,' she said, teasing him.

He slid his hands round her neck, under her dark hair, and drew her mouth towards him. 'He didn't know how long I'd been waiting for you,' he murmured against her lips.

His mouth travelled down her cheek to nuzzle into her neck, and she felt the familiar stirring inside and pressed against him. But he put her away from him, pulling a reluctant face. 'Duty calls, I'd better get back to the bank and catch up on what's been happening.'

'Yes, of course.' Lucie fought down the disappointment. This was how it would be from now on. Guy was an important man of business. It would have been wonderful if she could have believed that she came first with him, but she couldn't.

He was locking up his briefcase. 'You'll be OK?' he said rather absently.

'Oh yes.' She smiled brightly. 'I shall go shopping. I'm anxious to show off my cooking. All I've done up to now is open tins. I mean to tame the microwave oven this evening.'

'Fair enough,' said Guy. 'I'll drop you off in Georgetown and you can get a taxi back.'

In Comart, a mini-supermarket in the centre of the town, Lucie encountered Dorothy Maddox, all plump bronzed skin and sun-bleached hair, wearing a minuscule pink and white sundress.

She beamed all over her pleasant face. 'Hi, Lucie, you're back—we hoped we might meet up again before we left. We're going home tomorrow.' She kissed Lucie affectionately and held her away, inspecting her. 'You look lovely—and what a super tan you'll have to take back to England with you! We heard from Cynthia Blunt that you and Guy had gone to Little Cayman. The Blunts have rented a villa just along from us. He seems nice, but she's a bit—well, I'd call her a man's woman, if you know what I mean.' Dorothy trilled with laughter. 'Oh dear, I gossip too much! Look, my dear, I'm meeting Steve at the Conch Shell and I'm sure he'll love to see you again before we go. Pop your shopping in our car and let's have a soda while we wait for him.'

They were starting on their second soda when Steve arrived. 'Hi, Lucie girl, and how's the little ride?' He kissed her and sank into a chair, mopping his brow.

Dorothy pressed Lucie's hand. 'Doesn't she look lovely, Steve? Guy's a lucky man.' She slid Lucie a wicked glance. 'And I guess you're a lucky girl to get a man like that for yourself. He's out of this world! I said to Steve you both looked so *gorgeous* when you were taking your vows. I was in tears, and I haven't wept since my own eldest girl was married.'

Suddenly she clapped a hand to her cheek. 'Steve, I've just remembered. I must go back to the shops, I've forgotten my flying pills—you know I daren't fly without them.'

'Yes, dear. Would you like me to get them for you?' her husband offered without much enthusiasm.

'No, you stop and talk to Lucie. I won't be long. Can we give you a lift back to your apartment with your shopping, Lucie? If you're not meeting Guy.'

Lucie pulled a face. ''Fraid not. Guy's back on the old treadmill. He's at the bank.'

'What—already?' said Steve as his wife tripped away. 'That man's a workaholic!'

'That's what I'm afraid of,' Lucie said, and they both laughed, but she wondered if, perhaps, Steve was right. It didn't really matter any more, she thought. She could live happily in Guy's world of finance and big business. She could live happily in any world, just so long as he was in it.

Steve got up and fetched a soda for himself and slipped into the seat beside Lucie, leaning towards

her confidentially. 'Lucie, there's—er—there's jus
something I wanted to say to you while we're alone.
hope you don't mind.' He ran a finger round th
collar of his jazzy shirt. His face was pink and shiny
and he looked the picture of embarrassment.

'Yes?' Lucie raised her eyebrows encouragingly

He cleared his throat. 'Dorothy thinks I shouldn'
say this to you, but she doesn't understand how I feel
You see, Lucie, I like you and I guess I don't wan
you to feel bad about me. It's been on my mind an
I've had an idea that you might be blaming me.'

'Blaming you? Whatever for? You've been won
derful friends, you and Dorothy.'

Steve shook his head miserably. 'If I'd only
known——' He paused, eyeing her. 'You did know
didn't you, about the doctor's evidence—that you
father had a serious heart condition? That h
certainly shouldn't have been diving.'

Lucie stared at him blankly. She shook her head
slowly. 'No, nobody told me. Guy didn't want me t
go to the inquest, he said it would only upset me.

He stared at her, horrified. 'You didn't know
Then perhaps I shouldn't have said anything. But
wanted you to know that if I'd known about it I'
never had let him dive that day.' He took out
handkerchief and passed it over his moist brow. '
feel very bad about it. It's selfish of me to bring thi
up—and when you've just come back from you
honeymoon, too.'

He looked so embarrassed and unhappy that Luci
said automatically, 'You mustn't worry, Steve. It's al

n the past now and it wasn't your fault. You mustn't
blame yourself.'

He pressed her hand gratefully. 'You're a dear girl,
Lucie. Thank you, my dear, you've taken a weight
off my mind.' He glanced over his shoulder. 'Oh,
here's Dorothy now, you won't——'

'I won't give it another thought,' Lucie promised.
And knew that she could never keep that promise.
This was something that she couldn't put behind her.
Something that loomed up, black and forbidding,
full of dark warnings that she couldn't put a name to.

After the Maddoxes had driven her back to the
apartment and said their goodbyes, brimming over
with invitations and plans to meet again next year,
Lucie slumped into a chair and stared out at the blue,
innocent-looking sea. Accidental death, the verdict
had been, James had told her that much.

But *had* it been an accident? She heard her father's
voice again. 'Down there you're in another world—a
wonderful deep blue world—you forget all your
worries.' He must have had so many worries, so
much to forget. Her heart contracted. Had he sunk
down—down—deeper than a man who knew his
heart wouldn't stand the strain should venture—
knowing that he wouldn't come up again alive? Had
he chosen this way out when he knew, finally and
irrevocably, that the bank wasn't prepared to help
him any longer?

Lucie bit her lip hard, staring blindly out of the
window, and the beautiful calm view of sea and sand
swam before her eyes.

She had to know, she couldn't keep this suspicion
to herself. Guy, then? There was no one else to ask.
She had to find out whether Guy had signed her
father's death warrant.

CHAPTER SEVEN

SHE couldn't just sit here brooding for the rest of the afternoon. She had no appetite for lunch, so she set to and unpacked her boxes of food in the kitchen and started to plan a meal for this evening, trying to keep her mind on what she was doing. There was an instruction and recipe book on top of the sophisticated microwave oven, and she pored over it, concentrating resolutely on every detail. *Canard à l'orange* should be possible. With an exotic salad. Then cheese, sandwiched between courses in the French fashion, the way that Guy liked it, followed by fresh fruit, with coffee afterwards.

After the meal they would sit relaxed and watch the sunset and she would bring up the question that was nagging at her. She would say casually, 'I've been a bit bothered, darling. I met Steve Maddox today and he happened to mention something that threw me, rather. He said that it came out at the inquest that my father had a serious heart condition—that he shouldn't have been diving. I couldn't help wondering if he knew, if it was his way of—well, of getting out of a hopeless situation.'

They would discuss it quite calmly. Perhaps Guy would have something new to add, something that would set her mind at rest. She would tell him how she had quarrelled with her father years ago; how

nearly they had come to regaining the love they ha
once shared long ago; how much she grieved for hi
and that they had been denied that happiness. Ol
there was so much she could explain that she ha
never discussed with Guy. He knew nothing abou
her and her life. *No past—no future—just today*, h
had insisted on that first day of their honeymoo
and that was how it had been. Just the magica
happiness of each moment together as it came.

But now they were back in the real world wit
problems to face, and so long as they shared th
problems they could build a wonderful life togethe
She was sure it would happen. She would *make*
happen.

Preparations for dinner complete and everythin
tucked away in the fridge, Lucie poured herself a
ice-cold pineapple drink and took it back to th
verandah, with a box of biscuits. It was very hot ou
there, she should really go inside and switch on th
fan and lie on the bed and rest. But she was too jitter
to rest. She knew she wouldn't be able to relax unt
she had talked to Guy about Steve Maddox'
disclosure this morning. She closed her eyes agains
the sunlight filtering through the branches of th
palm-trees that overhung the verandah and tried t
stop thinking, and presently the stillness and the hea
lulled her into a light sleep.

A movement in front of the verandah brought he
wide awake. Guy, she thought, and her heart leap
But it was Cynthia Blunt who was strolling up th
beach towards her, looking exquisite in a whit
bikini with a scarlet cotton skirt tied at the waist an

hanging open at the front. She wore huge sun-glasses and an enormous straw hat and her silky skin was tanned to a biscuit-brown perfection.

She climbed the steps on to the verandah, uninvited, and sank down into one of the blue canvas loungers. 'Hello, and how's the little bride today? Enjoyed your honeymoon?'

Lucie felt the adrenalin begin to flow. 'Honeymoons are always enjoyable, don't you think?' she said coolly.

Cynthia took off her hat and laid her head against the back of the chair. Her hair was white-gold, drawn back from her face in the way that only ballet dancers and women who are completely sure of their own beauty can afford to do. 'Ah yes,' she sighed. 'Such a pity the dream has to end.'

'Is it?' murmured Lucie. If she thinks I'm going to be frightened by her stupid innuendoes she can think again, she thought. But suddenly the picture of Guy and this woman strolling along beside the harbour, arms linked, on the day of the wedding appeared before her eyes.

'Oh, yes.' The other woman turned her enormous sun-glasses on Lucie. 'That's what I came to warn you about, my child, just in case Guy doesn't see fit to. Men are sometimes stupidly devious about these things, but we women have to be perfectly honest with each other—if not with the men. Don't you agree?'

She waited, smiling thin-lipped, and when Lucie remained silent, she went on, 'I think I must explain the position to you, my poor dear Lucie. You're very

young, but I don't think you're a fool, so you would
probably guess the truth before long yourself, but I'm
doing you a favour by putting you in the picture so
that you're forearmed. The fact is that Guy and I
have been lovers for some time, and neither of us
wishes to make any change. At the moment it suits
him to have a wife. Now that he's chairman of the
bank he needs a certain—er—cloak of respect-
ability. You, my dear Lucie, are that cloak, if you get
my meaning. However, my husband and I will be
divorcing before long, and after that Guy will no
doubt arrange to get his freedom too. But until then
he'll probably need to keep you on for a short time.
And if you want your little bit of fun with him during
that time I shan't make a fuss about it. After all, Guy
and I will have the rest of our lives together.'

Lucie was on her feet, one hand gripping the
balcony rail. She stared at the woman lounging back
in the chair, as if she were confronting a venomous
snake. Her knees were trembling and she felt sick,
but she said quite steadily, 'I don't believe you. And
please go now.'

Cynthia Blunt rose gracefully. 'Of course,' she said
silkily. 'I hardly expected you to believe me, you poor
child. And if you choose to tackle Guy he'll probably
deny it. But if you need proof, Guy will be at the villa
with me this afternoon. We can't wait to get together
again. My dear husband has an important meeting
with some of the other lawyers in your father's case.
Call in around three o'clock—I think you'll be
convinced.' She replaced her hat with a languid
gesture and glanced at the slim gold watch on her

wrist. 'I must get back—I wouldn't want to keep Guy waiting, would I?' Still smiling, she strolled away along the beach.

Lucie stared after her, her throat constricted. She was lying, of course she was. A beastly woman, out to make trouble. Bored with her husband, jealous of a younger woman. Perhaps she had tried to get Guy and failed. Yes, that would make a woman like that livid with jealousy.

Perhaps—Lucie faced it. Perhaps she and Guy *had* been lovers once. A long time ago. She began to shiver in the hot sunshine.

She went into the apartment and paced up and down the long living-room. She wouldn't go, of course she wouldn't, she trusted Guy. If only Dorothy hadn't told her where the Blunts were now living she *couldn't* go, because she wouldn't know where to go to. But Dorothy *had* told her. 'The Blunts have rented a villa just along from us,' Dorothy had said this morning. That meant that it was in the same complex as Lucie's father's villa. Just five or six minutes' walk along the beach.

'No,' she said aloud. 'I won't go. I won't, I won't!' She looked at her watch. It was half-past one. She had to get through the time until Guy came back, and she didn't know when that would be. It would all depend on how much work he had found waiting for him.

She went into her bedroom, the one she had slept in since Guy brought her here a fortnight ago. Tonight he would join her here and they would make love, and she would—what would she do? Would she

tell him about Cynthia Blunt's visit? Better not to
better to put the whole thing aside just as you drop an
unwanted advertisement in the waste basket and
never give it another thought.

She would arrange for maid service tomorrow, but
for today she would prepare the bedroom herself
She found clean linen, stripped the bed and fitted th
green bottom sheet without a wrinkle, changed the
pillow-cases, persuaded the duvet into its patterned
cover. Not that they would need it tonight, it was
going to be a warm night. Just a sheet would do.

She fetched Guy's brushes and combs and lotion
from his room and laid them beside her own on th
dressing-counter, holding the shiny back of th
tortoiseshell brush against her cheek. He had used it
in the shack and she could see him now so clearly
standing by the long window looking out at the sea
brushing back his dark hair, while she lay on the air
bed, watching him lazily, waiting for him to turn and
come over and take her in his arms—— She replaced
the brush. Somehow, at this moment, she didn't
want to remember.

The room had gathered a little dust while they
were away. She flicked it round and made sure that
the shower-room was spotless. Then she looked a
her watch and saw with surprise that only half an
hour had passed.

She got into a bikini and walked down to the sea
The water was tepid and licked round her ankles
and she spent another half-hour swimming in the
shallows, watching the tiny darting fish below in the
clear water. Tomorrow she would go into George

town and see if she could buy paints and brushes, it would be fun to start to make some sketches for her new book, and it would pass the time while Guy was busy at the bank, before they flew back to London and her new life.

She sat on the warm, soft sand, while a group of children played round her with a large striped red and white ball, and tried to imagine what her life would be like. True to his decision, Guy had told her nothing of it—she didn't even know where they would live. Their honeymoon had been, as he had wished, a matter of living for the moment. It would be fun, finding out all about each other. Most couples do that when they become engaged—talking endlessly, making plans together. They had all that excitement to come.

She shivered and realised that a bank of clouds had come up and obscured the sun. Was it going to thunder? She didn't think they had thunderstorms here at this time of the year, but there was a first time for everything. She went inside the villa and showered and dressed in one of the simple cotton dresses she had brought with her. She towelled her hair and brushed it dry, then looked at her watch again. It said seven minutes to three.

Her heart started to beat heavily. If she walked along the beach—just a little way? She could do something that she had put off until now—call in at her father's villa. There would be a lot to do there, sorting out all his things. It would be an opportunity to see what state the villa was in after having been shut up.

And perhaps she would see Cynthia Blunt
sunbathing on the verandah of one of the other
villas—alone. Or sipping an aperitif with some of the
other residents as they lounged on the patio that
surrounded the pool? And then she would know for
sure that the woman had been lying.

For a long, long minute she stood in the bedroom
and her breath seemed to be hurting her chest. Then
she went out, as if drawn by a magnet, and started to
walk quickly along the beach, in the shade of the
trees.

The first rumble of thunder sounded as she
reached the group of white villas with the steeply-
sloping pink roofs. The second one, standing back a
little, was where her father had lived, where she had
met him again.

Suddenly the storm broke with tropical violence.
Lucie made a dash for the verandah of the villa, but
the rain was beating in from the sea and there was no
shelter on the verandah. She tried the long glass door
into the living-room. It was unlocked, and she went
inside and pulled it to.

In the big room nothing had changed except that
there was a thin film of dust over everything, giving
the place a neglected, pathetic look. Her father's big
desk in the corner still had a pile of his papers on it,
under a big conch-shell paperweight. He had been
coming back that day for a meeting with Guy—but
he had never come back.

Lucie's eyes filled with tears, remembering the last
time she had seen him, how he had taken her in his
arms and kissed her. It had been a reconciliation of

uch promise. If only they had had more time ogether——.

She stood looking out of the big picture window as he storm raged. Lucie had never been afraid of hunder, and she watched the swirling rain with a kind of fascination. As soon as the storm was over he would go back. She should never have come this ar; she should never have given another thought to he lies of a vicious, jealous woman. She loved Guy and she must believe that he loved her. So many memories of his lovemaking, of his tenderness for her, of his obvious happiness on their island honeymoon, came back to her as she stood at the window, and her mouth softened into a smile as she remembered.

The adjoining villa was the one belonging to Steve and Dorothy Maddox. Beyond that, and standing at an angle, overhung by a huge palm tree, was the third in the complex. Was that where the Blunts were living? A car was parked at one side under the tree. A dark-coloured car.

Lucie caught her breath. Not Guy's car? The window was blurred and misty and she rubbed it with the palm of her hand, peering out. It could equally well be another hired car, she told herself, one of the same make. It meant nothing, nothing at all.

Then a man appeared on the verandah, looking back to speak to someone inside the villa. Lucie froze. Even at this distance Guy was unmistakable, she knew every inch of him, the way he stood, the way he moved, the height and darkness of him. He

lifted a hand as if in farewell, then a woma
appeared, wearing some floating white garmen
and, apparently oblivious of the rain, flung her arm
round the man's neck, clinging to him as if partin
was agony. Their bodies were locked together in
long, long lovers' kiss.

Lucie closed her eyes and gripped the met
handle of the door as nausea struck. She lurche
across the room and into the bathroom and wa
horribly sick.

Later, somehow, she dragged herself back alon
the sodden beach. The storm had passed over now
but the palm trees dripped coldly on her head an
shoulders. She couldn't stop shivering and her leg
felt as if they didn't belong to her.

Back at the condo she stripped off her soakin
garments and got under a hot shower. She mustn'
get ill—not now when there was so much to do. Sh
towelled dry and got into jeans and a jumper an
went to the telephone to look up the number of th
airport, turning over the pages feverishly, bent o
only one thing—to get away from here as quickly a
possible. If Guy wasn't back before she left sh
would ring his office at the bank and tell him she wa
going.

Yes, there was a seat on the flight leaving fo
Miami at five-forty. It seemed as if Fate were on he
side, helping her once again to escape from a
intolerable situation. She rang the taxi firm an
booked a car, then started to pack her bag.

Guy returned before she had finished.

'What are you doing?' He stood in the doorway

ery straight. For a fleeting moment Lucie thought
e looked like a man facing a firing squad, but that
as just her imagination, of course.

'I'm leaving,' she said. 'There doesn't seem much
oint in staying on here, and I want to get back to my
ork. I've got my return flight back to England,
nd——'

'Work?' he broke in. 'What work?'

She folded a woollen jumper neatly and laid it on
op of her case. It would be cold back in the flat in
ondon. 'I'm an artist of sorts,' she said. 'Didn't I
ention it?'

'No,' he said, 'you didn't. Why didn't you?'

'I suppose I didn't think it would be of much
iterest to a chairman of a bank,' she said coolly, and
w the way his mouth tightened at the jibe. 'But I've
ad a small success in my own way. I've had a
hildren's book published and another one accepted,
 come out later this year. I want to get going on my
ext one. I have a studio flat, you know, where I
ved and worked before—before you blackmailed
e into marriage. I've left the address beside the
lephone where you can get in touch with me later.
.s I don't intend to go on with this marriage any
nger I shall go back to the flat, to live and work.'

Guy crossed the room in two strides. His face was
ark with anger, the blue eyes pierced like steel
lades. 'The hell you will!' he forced the words
etween his teeth. 'You're my wife and you stay here
ith me. I need you.'

Of course you do, she thought bitterly. If it wasn't
or me your best friend might begin to wonder what

was going on between you and his wife.

He lowered his voice and said, 'What's got int
you, Lucie? I thought you understood—I've got a bi
job to do—responsibilities——' He ran a han
through his smooth dark hair, ruffling it until it stoc
up in little peaks. Oh God, Lucie thought wildl
staring at it. I want to feel his hair under my fingers,
want to throw myself in his arms and tell him I lov
him and long for him and I don't care about anythin
so long as I can stay in his life, in his bed——

I mustn't, I mustn't, she thought desperately, an
pushed down the lid of her case. 'I always told you
hated your way of life, and now I see for myself a
that it leads to. Money—deals—manipulating pe
ple—that's all that you think about, and it's—it
callous—heartless——' She choked over the fin:
word.

'Lucie, this is crazy! I don't recognise myself i
what you're saying——'

'Don't you?' She closed her hands over the back (
a chair and stared up at him with accusing eye
'What about my father? Why didn't you tell me th:
it came out at the enquiry that he had a serious hea
condition? I had to hear about it from Stev
Maddox!'

Puzzledly he said, 'James and I agreed that then
was no point in your knowing that and——'

'No point!' Her voice rose tremblingly. 'Of cour:
there was a point. You could have helped him—he'
relied on your bank for years—but you refused.'

He clicked his tongue in exasperation. 'My de:
girl, you don't know what you're talking abou

There's a limit to what any bank can do for a customer. Your father owed us millions—there wasn't a chance in hell that he could have ever repaid us.'

She went on stonily, as if he hadn't spoken. 'He must have been at the end of his tether when he went down on that dive. He must have known that he wouldn't come up again——'

Guy's face was ashen. 'Great God, Lucie, what are you saying?'

'I'm saying that if it hadn't been for you my father might have been alive today!'

'And that's why you want to leave?' His voice was dangerously quiet now.

'Partly,' she said, biting her lip hard.

'And may I enquire what the other part is?' He was at his most sarcastic. Lucie hated his sarcasm, it made her cringe inside. But she had started this now and she must go on.

She said, 'I know now why you wanted to marry me, and it's squalid and beastly.'

He said very quietly, 'Perhaps you'll be good enough to explain.'

'You and Cynthia Blunt, of course. I saw you together down by the harbour, the day of our wedding, when you said you had work to do—and I couldn't help wondering then—but I told myself not to be silly and suspicious. But Cynthia herself came to see me today. She told me that you and she had been lovers for some time and intended not to make any change.'

'And you believed her?' he said icily.

'I—I didn't know,' she faltered. 'It seemed to—to fit in.'

'To fit in with what?'

'I know that people like you think nothing of it—it's all part of your life-style—having a wife and a mistress—but I think it's degrading and I refuse to be—to be used like this. She said she and her husband were divorcing soon and then you wouldn't need me as a—a cover-up.'

She stopped, trying to find some message in the hard, expressionless face, but he was looking at her as if she were a stranger. Oh, please say something, she willed him desperately. Deny it, or admit it or explain. Just say *something*!

'I didn't want to believe her,' she rushed on, and now the words seemed to be pouring out of her. She had a terrible feeling that she was losing him, but she couldn't stop. 'But I was on the beach this afternoon—I went into my father's villa to shelter from the storm, and I saw you and her together—she was in your arms——'

'You were spying on me?' She flinched at the contempt in his voice.

'No, I——'

'That's enough!' Guy lifted a hand and she thought he was going to strike her, but it dropped to his side again and his words, when they came, had a cold finality that was more frightening than any anger would have been. 'So that's what you think of me?' His face was a hard mask. She felt that it was a stranger standing before her. 'Of course you wouldn't want to remain married to a blackmailer

nd a murderer and an adulterer, would you? So you
nay as well go. Go back to your bedsitter and paint
our little pictures. Go quickly—now, and don't
ome back!' He turned and strode out of the room,
nd the violent slamming of the door was the only
ign of the rage that she had seen ready to erupt
nside him.

She heard the engine of the hired car, the squeal of
rakes as he pulled up at the entrance to the road.
hen the noise dying away.

ater that day mist lay over the island as the plane
ose into the evening sky, and all Lucie could see as
he looked down was a vague, greenish shape. Her
ast thought before it disappeared altogether was, 'I
vonder what will happen to the *Canard à l'orange*.'
And then she began to weep.

ondon was grey and bitterly cold. The last of the
now still lay in dirty piles in corners. The flat was
hilly and unwelcoming and the African violet in its
ot on the windowsill was past hope. Lucie lit the gas
re and made tea, then pulled up a chair and sat,
eeling utterly dejected and hopeless. Less than three
veeks since she had left here: it seemed impossible
hat so much happiness and so much misery could be
rammed into three short weeks. But she must try to
ut it behind her now. She would go to ground here
nd work—work—work. Always before, her remedy
gainst depression and loneliness had been her work.
Jow, more than ever, it must come to her help.

She wondered whether to let James know she had

come back, but she couldn't face his surprise, hi
worried questioning. Sooner or later he would hav
to know, but not yet. She would get into her wor
first, that would turn her into a human being again

The appalling fact, which began to dawn on he
days later, was that her work wasn't going to hel
this time. She had planned to paint the tiny coloure
fishes against their home of coral, but that was out c
the question. She would have to think of somethin
that didn't remind her of Guy and their honeymoo
island. But nothing came, and her pencil refused t
draw even a doodle that might turn into somethin
interesting, and the floor heaped up with crumple
sheets of discarded paper.

From the moment she had run away in the stor
from the sight of that woman in Guy's arms she ha
ceased to think. She had lashed out blindly agains
him, wanting to hurt him as much as he had hurt hei
She had left him without even beginning to think th
thing through.

But now she couldn't stop thinking. The thought
scurried round in her brain like ants all day and mos
of the night. Perhaps he could have explained abou
Cynthia, but she hadn't given him a chance. O
could it possibly not have been Cynthia and Guy a
all, but two other people? The rain had been sheetin
down, blurring their figures. Had her suspicion
made her imagine something quite, quite wrong?

And she had practically accused him of bein
responsible for her father's death. What a dreadfi
thing to do! No wonder he had looked at her as if sh
disgusted him. Of course he wasn't responsible, b

was only doing his job. The fact that she was prejudiced against everything in the world of big business, of which he was a part, was no excuse for making such a terrible suggestion.

He wouldn't forgive her, ever. 'Get out of my life,' he had said, coldly and contemptuously, and he had meant it. His face, white with rage and disgust, haunted her every moment. Surely, though, he would have to get in touch with her soon?

He didn't get in touch. Day after endless day she sat alone in the flat with a blank sheet of paper in front of her, creeping out only to buy food that she couldn't eat, lying awake at night until her misery pressed on her like a great lump of stone, and finally she buried her head in the pillow and wept. But the days passed and there was no letter, no phone call for her, although she left her door open all the time in case the phone rang in the hall below.

It was eleven days after her return when she heard a man's step on the stairs, and her heart almost stopped beating. The door was pushed further open and a voice said, 'Lucie? Is this the right place?'

Not Guy's voice. All her breath left her in a long sigh.

Giles Blunt was standing in the doorway. 'I am right, then. Hello, Lucie, may I come in?'

He had come from Guy, of course he had. The bank's lawyer. He had come to discuss proceedings for the divorce.

'Yes—what a surprise! Do come in and sit down.' Her voice was high and uneven. She pulled out a chair for him and he sat down, his thin, clever face faintly embarrassed. 'Can I get you anything? A drink?'

'No, thanks.' He looked down at his shoes. 'I've come on a rather strange errand, Lucie. I'm not sure if I'll be welcome.'

She was icy cold now. 'Of course you are. How are you?'

'I'm fine,' he said, and waited a moment. 'It's Guy, you see. In a way I'm here on his behalf, if that doesn't sound strange.'

'Not at all,' she said politely. From a lawyer, come to arrange a divorce, the wording might be correct.

'How is he?' she heard herself ask. You were dying and yet you could keep up a conversation like this. It was very odd.

'Much better,' said Giles. 'He's out of hospital now and back at the condo, but you know, Lucie, I really think he needs looking after. He knows you left Grand Cayman because you have a deadline for your next book and he made me promise not to tell you about his accident in case you worried, but——'

'No!' her hand went to her throat. 'What accident? I didn't know——'

Giles looked surprised and more embarrassed than ever. 'Oh lord, have I really put my foot in it? I thought you'd have been notified.'

She shook her head numbly. 'What happened?'

He was regarding her rather strangely. 'In his car—about ten days ago. The usual thing—someone just in from Europe forgot that you drive on the left in the Caymans. Guy's usually wary about that, but this time his concentration must have slipped a bit

He sheered off the road and the car hit a tree. He was lucky, actually. Slight concussion and a broken left wrist. The usual bruises, but nothing really serious. He says he's going back to work on Monday, but I don't think he's fit really. He looks pretty low. I've left my partner out in the Caymans and as I was coming back to London I thought I'd drop in and tell you the score.'

Lucie licked her dry lips. 'Guy didn't ask you to see me?'

'No, he didn't. He says he's quite OK and there's no reason to take you away from your work. I expect that's why he didn't want you to know.'

But a newly-married couple would be in touch every day, as a matter of course. So why hadn't she bothered to find out what was happening when she didn't hear from him? She could almost see the question posing itself behind Giles Blunt's clever grey eyes.

She shook her head helplessly. 'That wasn't the reason, Giles. You may as well know—Guy and I have split up.'

'So soon?' he said, but she could see that that was what he had guessed.

'Yes,' she muttered, clenching her fists to stop herself from breaking down. 'The shortest marriage on record,' she said bitterly.

There was a long, uncomfortable silence. Giles broke it at last. 'I'm sorry, Lucie, it's pure hell, isn't t? Fellow-feeling, you know,' he added, looking out f the window at the tall houses opposite. 'I'm in the ame boat myself—my own marriage has come to an nd, finally. Cynthia came back to London with me—unwillingly—but tomorrow we both see our solicitors. So that's that,' he added grimly. 'We join the club.' He stood up. 'I'm not going to stay and play for sympathy, Lucie. These things happen and we have to get over them.' He walked to the door. 'But I'm glad I came. At least you know the score now and you can do what you think best. It was wrong of Guy not to let you know, and I'm not going to apologise for going behind his back and coming to see you.'

He held out a hand and looked deeply into her eyes. 'Good luck, Lucie. Guy's a fine chap and you're a very nice girl. I only hope the two of you can work something out.'

'Thank you,' she whispered, putting her hand in his. 'And thank you for coming.'

When Giles had gone Lucie took out her building society book and turned over the pages with shaking fingers. Then she pulled on a mac and went out to catch a bus to the West End. Here she found the agents that she and Peter had dealt with before. I' she used every penny she possessed, including wha' was left of her advance from the publishers, she could afford a return ticket to Grand Cayman. She would probably have to wait three days for a flight the exquisite young lady behind the desk told her

'Oh, isn't there anything sooner?' Lucie wailed 'Please, couldn't there possibly be a cancellation o something?'

'We-ell.' The clerk looked with faint interest at th white face of the girl before her. 'Urgent, is it?'

'It's my husband,' Lucie swallowed hard. 'He's ou

there on business and he's—he's had an accident.'

'Oh, too bad!' The girl's maroon-tipped fingers fluttered over the booking records. 'There *might* just be one seat on a flight via Houston tomorrow morning. We're waiting for confirmation now. Would you like to sit down, and I'll try to get in touch.'

'Oh, *thank* you.' Lucie shrank into a huge soft lounge-seat and prayed hard.

God was listening at last. Next morning Lucie was in the huge jet that rose into the air from Heathrow, en route for Houston, Texas, USA.

Guy would reject her again—why should he want her when Cynthia was going to be free? But that didn't seem to matter now. All that mattered was that she should see him again, and the need was a physical pain inside her.

She laid her head back and closed her eyes and pictured his face close to hers after they had made love on their honeymoon island. Saw the way his blue eyes were soft and his mouth relaxed into happiness, felt the weight of his arm flung across her body as if he didn't want to let her go. He *had* felt something for her more than just physical need, she tried to persuade herself.

But the conviction that she was embarking on a fool's errand was heavy inside her.

CHAPTER EIGHT

THE flight went on and on endlessly. Lucie couldn't sleep, couldn't relax, but the need for sleep burned behind her eyelids. In the transit lounge at Houston she drank black coffee in case she fell asleep at last and missed her connecting flight to Grand Cayman. She needn't have worried, she was wide awake when her flight was called, and three and a half hours later she was back in the familiar Owen Roberts Airport and her nerves were at screaming-point.

Time had dragged on the flight, but now it was racing. When the taxi reached the entrance to the condo complex she nearly panicked and told the driver to turn round and take her back. She tapped him on the shoulder. 'Put me down here, please.'

The man turned good humouredly. 'No cause walk round in the dark, miss, I can drive you.'

'Thanks, but I want to walk,' Lucie muttered fishing in her purse for the fare.

It was indeed dark—nearly ten o'clock loca time—and the sky was cloudy. No stars, no moon Lucie picked up her bag and set off along the smooth drive leading to the group of condominiums over looking the sea. Her legs were stiff with sitting for all those hours in the plane, her knees were shaking so much that she could hardly walk, and once she lurched sideways and nearly ended up in the bushes Lights were shining in some of the windows of the low white buildings. She looked up at the first-floor apartment of the second building. Yes, there was a light, so Guy must be there. She went hollow inside. By the time she had circled the swimming-pool she had to summon all the will-power she had left not to turn and run as she stood before the door, her hands clammy and her heart beating in her throat. No, she told herself. You've run away twice, this time you stay and face reality.

Mercifully the bottom door was unlocked, and she climbed the stairs to the first floor and stopped before the familiar blue-painted door. What if Guy wasn't alone? He might have one of his business friends with him, and that would be horribly embarrassing. But at least she knew that Cynthia Blunt wasn't here, because Giles had said she had gone back to London with him.

Holding her breath, she pushed open the door and went into the small, square hall.

'Who's that?' Guy's voice came from the bedroom.

'It's me, Lucie,' she croaked.

He appeared in the bedroom doorway. He was wearing the crimson silk gown that she remembered so well, and it accentuated the pallor of his face. He had lost weight and he looked taller. There were great dark circles under his eyes and his hair was rumpled and spiky. One wrist was heavily bandaged.

They stared at each other, then Guy made a helpless gesture. 'You'd better come in.' He led the way into the living-room and switched on the light. 'Sit down,' he said, and she sat in one corner of the sofa.

He stood looking down at her, his face expressionless. There was a long silence, then he said, 'So you came back.'

'Yes,' said Lucie.

'Why?' He was wary, suspicious.

She had rehearsed what she would say, gone over and over it in the plane, but now she couldn't remember a word. 'I heard you'd been ill and I had to see you again,' she said in a shaking voice.

'How did you know?' he asked matter-of-factly.

'Giles Blunt came to see me. He—he told me you'd been in an accident and had been in hospital. He said he thought you needed someone to look after you.'

Guy stood up and started to pace up and down the room. 'He'd no right to do that—it was none of his bloody business!'

Lucie's heart plummeted. He didn't want her here; this was all going terribly wrong. 'I think he meant it for the best,' she faltered. 'He didn't seem to know that things had—had gone wrong between us. He said you knew I had to get on with my work and you didn't want to worry me.' She clasped her hands tightly together. 'Guy—why didn't you send word to me? I'm your wife, I should have known.'

'Would you have cared?' he said bitterly. He came and stood in front of her again, his blue eyes cold and distant.

'Of course I would.'

His lip curled disdainfully. 'After the summing up of my character that you treated me to before you made your exit I could hardly expect that you'd take the slightest interest in my welfare.'

'Oh, Guy—don't be like that, please don't. Let me explain——'

'Go on then, explain,' he said coldly. He walked away and stood staring out of the uncurtained window at the darkness outside.

She looked at the tall, uncompromising back. The crimson silk of his robe reached to his thighs; below it his legs were straight and muscular, the springy hair dark against the bronzed skin, and Lucie thought despairingly that she had never loved him so much as at this time when she had finally lost him. She wasn't a very brave person and it took all her courage to get up and stand beside him and say, 'I was wrong and unfair. I was insanely jealous of Cynthia Blunt and I just said the first thing that came into my mind. I'm sorry.'

Guy turned slowly. 'You were—jealous? Is that what you said?' He spun round, looking as if he couldn't believe what he had heard.

'Of course I was jealous,' Lucie said almost crossly. 'Wouldn't any girl be jealous when she's just seen the man she loved with another woman in his arms?'

'Did you say—the man she loved? Was that what you said? Are you saying you love me, Lucie?'

It wasn't so hard now. Something in his face, in his voice, was sending a little tremor of hope into her misery. She put a hand on his arm. 'I love you, Guy, and I don't care about anything else, and I won't give you up to Cynthia Blunt, so that's that!'

Incredibly, he was laughing, a broken sort of laugh. 'Oh, my darling, darling, fierce little Lucie, how I adore you! I've dreamed of hearing you say you loved me, and I was beginning to believe it would never happen.'

'Then—then you don't want Cynthia?'

'I want Cynthia as much as I want a 'flu virus. I've been trying for the last six months to get her out of my hair. That day I'd gone to see her, at my request. I wanted to plead with her to treat Giles with some decency. He still loves her, the poor old idiot. It didn't do any good, of course. She put on her usual act, even to the point of rushing out into the storm after me and throwing herself into my arms. That must have been the great dramatic climax that you witnessed.'

Suddenly his face changed. 'It's you I want, my love. It's always been you. God, Lucie, if you only knew how much I want you! I've loved you for years.'

She looked into the blue eyes that blazed with love and tenderness and she knew that, unbelievable as it seemed, it was true. She caught her breath as she leaned towards him, and then, somehow, they were together on the sofa and his good arm was round her and his heart was pounding against hers.

'Tell me,' she whispered, holding up her mouth.

Against her lips, between kisses, he told her. 'Beautiful, adorable Lucie, I love you to distraction and I want you with me always, to the end of time. When you went away my world went black. But I'm only a man, and I could show you better than ever I could tell you.'

His kisses were driving her mad. 'I'm reeling with jet-lag and you're just out of hospital. Could we? Should we? Your wrist——?'

Guy drew her to her feet and towards th

bedroom. 'We could,' he said masterfully, 'and we should. And it isn't my wrist I propose to use,' he added wickedly.

They sat on the bed together. 'You can be nurse and undress me,' he teased, his blue eyes dancing, so she did just that, and when it was done she revelled in the bronzed strength of his spare, muscular body as he lay waiting for her.

'Hurry, my lovely love,' he smiled at her as she began to pull off her own clothes, and the blaze of love and satisfaction in his face made her almost shy as the last flimsy garment was cast aside.

'I was so afraid,' she murmured as she lay down beside him and turned herself to meet him. 'I thought we'd never do this again.'

'Over and over again, I promise you,' he said triumphantly, his one good hand exploring and caressing and rousing her to a wild, reckless response, 'and it will get better and better all the time.'

As their lips met frenziedly and they moved together to the final peak of ecstasy, Lucie cried out his name over and over. His head was pressed into the hollow of her neck and she heard him groan, 'Lucie—my darling—oh God—Lucie——'

Afterwards they lay still, and for Lucie the world slid away into a beautifully peaceful nothingness. For a little while she slept, and when she woke it was to see Guy propped on one elbow, looking down at her.

'I don't believe it,' he said. 'I'd given it up as hopeless, and suddenly—you're here. You are real, aren't you, Lucie?'

'Mm—I think so. I'm just beginning to believe it myself.' She snuggled up to him. 'The last week's been so ghastly. Did you really miss me?'

'Miss you? I bloody well did! I thought I'd lost you that day you walked out. I went a little mad, I think. I drove straight out and hit a tree.'

'Oh!' she wailed. 'That was my fault. Are you sure you're all right now? Oh, I've been so stupid, so incredibly silly!'

'Shush!' He covered her mouth with his own.

After a considerable time she said, 'Guy, we've got to talk.'

He sighed. 'Very well, but first things first. Let's have a celebration meal—I haven't had a square meal since you walked out on me.'

'Neither have I,' she admitted. 'And at this moment, I'm starving!' Suddenly she remembered. 'Did you find the duck thing I'd prepared ready to pop in the microwave?'

He nodded with a grin. 'That duck was a hostage to fortune. I tucked the whole thing away in the deep-freeze, in the remote hope that you'd come back to share it with me.'

'Marvellous! We'll have a gourmet supper ready in half an hour. I can't wait!'

Much later, they went out and strolled together dreamily along the edge of the sea, their arms round each other, as they had done every evening on their honeymoon. There was no moon yet and the sky was thick with stars. The beach was deserted except for the two of them and the only sounds were the splash of the waves and the rustle of the leaves in the pine trees, and the high-pitched twitter of night insects.

'Did you really mean it—that you'd loved me for years?' Lucie could still not quite believe it.

'Indeed I did,' said Guy, lowering his head to kiss her just above her ear. 'Three years ago, after that one and only time we met, I tried so hard to find you again, but I had to give up in the end. I even thought I'd forgotten you. But when I saw you again at your father's party it was like a blow over the heart. That night in Paris—I'd been looking at you all through dinner, fascinated. You were so incredibly beautiful, your hair like a dark cloud and your shoulders so white and that damnably seductive cleavage that I couldn't take my eyes off. And when you looked back at me I saw what I was sure was invitation in your face. It never occurred to me—stupid fool that I was—that Warren Martin's daughter could be innocent. I took you for twenty-three or four—your father was past middle age and that seemed to fit. And your dress—if you'll forgive me for saying so, sweetheart—was decidely—er—racy.'

Lucie grimaced. 'I know. Stephanie chose it for me and I loathed it. She'd just married Father and he wanted me off the scene as quickly as possible. I suppose she thought it would be alluring and put up my stock in the marriage market. I hated that dress, t seemed to label me as one of them, and that was the very last thing I wanted. I couldn't bear Father's set. They drank too much and talked about nothing but money and deals and take-overs, and their wives were so—so bored and snooty and didn't seem to are when their husbands pawed me and—oh, they were horrid!'

She sighed. 'And I looked at you and you were so handsome and—and different. I'd never seen anyone like you at my father's parties before. I suppose I was very young for my age and quite absurdly romantic. I began to build up all sorts of fantasies about falling in love and how we would kiss chastely among the roses and how you would swear eternal devotion.'

Guy let out a groan. 'God, yes—and then I came on too strong and frightened the life out of you!'

She giggled. 'And all because my dress was so alluring! Clothes have a lot to answer for. Stephanie must have been right after all.'

He stroked her neck. 'I certainly found it alluring, any man would, but there was no thought of wedding-bells in my mind. That came later.'

'When? How much later?'

'Very soon,' he said thoughtfully. 'You see, you gave me a terrific shock when you pushed me into the rose-bed and ran off. I was seething. Nothing like that had ever happened to me before. I was bigheaded about my technique with girls, and you gave my pride a very nasty jolt. I sat there and blasphemed very colourfully indeed. But after a while I got up and brushed myself down and told myself that it wasn't the end of the world. You were just a silly teenager, playing at being grown-up, and then, when it came to the crunch, too scared to accept what happens when you look at a man with those big eyes of yours in that special way.'

'Charming,' Lucie murmured. 'I really must have made an impression!'

He brushed his mouth against her hair again and

drew her closer, and she felt a tremor run through him. 'Oh, you did, my darling, indeed you did. That night I couldn't sleep for thinking about you. I kept seeing you in the moonlight in that rose-garden, with your lips quivering and your lovely face raised to mine so trustingly. Hearts-and-flowers stuff. All that was lacking was a violin playing off-stage. An innocent girl was something new to me, and I wanted you quite desperately. I was disgusted with the way I'd behaved. I got out of bed and drank several stiff drinks, but they didn't help me to go to sleep and forget all about you. They only made me want you more. By the time morning came I was hearing wedding-bells loud and clear and I was aching to see you again, to touch you, to ask you to forgive me for frightening you. I was all ready to ask your father for his daughter's hand in marriage and show him my bank account, as they did in the good old days.'

Lucie chuckled. 'And when you arrived you found I'd bolted. Did Father tell you why?'

He shook his head. 'I couldn't get anything out of him. He was not in a communicative mood, to put it mildly.'

'I can guess. I'd disobeyed him for the first time in my life and he was furious. I'd run away from the finishing school he'd chosen for me and I was determined to go to art school, which he was dead against. Also he was dropping dark hints about making a suitable marriage—and that meant setting out to capture you—the son of his banker. Very useful to him!' she giggled. 'I shan't tell you all the uncomplimentary things I said about you that night! Anyway, we had a flaming row and the next day I walked out and went to James, in Birmingham. That was the last time I saw my father until he wrote and asked me to come out to the Caymans and see him— three years later.'

'And all was forgiven and forgotten?'

She nodded sadly. 'I think he really wanted to see me and make up our quarrel.'

Guy squeezed her shoulder in sympathy. They were both silent for a while and the little waves broke at their feet and the moon came up and sent a white track across the sea.

Guy said slowly, 'I think you were wrong, you know, my love. I don't believe he wanted to die. He was a fighter, he would have gone on trying.'

'Oh, I hope so,' she said. 'But we'll never know, shall we?'

He shook his head. 'Perhaps not. And now we must go back and I shall put you to bed and let you sleep. And tomorrow we'll really start our life together.'

'That sounds like heaven,' said Lucie, reaching up to kiss him softly on the lips.

The following morning they had a very late and leisurely breakfast on the verandah. Lucie had never in her life imagined such bliss—the blue of the sea, the blue canopy of the sky above and the deeper blue of her husband's eyes smiling into hers across the table.

'I've got something to show you,' he said. 'Something that really you should have shown me.'

'Sounds mysterious,' Lucie murmured pouring out the last of the coffee.

He went inside and came back with a jiffy bag. 'This,' he said. 'I found it yesterday morning in your father's desk. I had to go along to look through some papers they were asking for at the bank.'

'My book!' gasped Lucie. 'Peter brought it for my father.'

Guy smiled broadly. 'Exactly. I'm very proud to have a famous author and illustrator for my wife. It's delightful, Lucie. You're extremely talented.'

She flushed with pleasure. 'An ill-favoured thing but mine own,' she said.

'You must go on with your art,' Guy said seriously. 'I'll have a studio fixed up for you at the cottage in Dorset and you can go there and paint whenever you feel inclined. It's a very nice cottage, I think you'll like it. Tucked away in woodlands, not far from the sea. The nearest thing I could get in England to the Little Cayman shack.' His eyes twinkled. 'We'll spend lots of time there when the pressure of London gets too much. You won't object to the flat in London?' he added anxiously. 'You won't hate my business friends if they're so misguided as to talk finance?'

Lucie pulled a wry face. 'I know I've been stupidly prejudiced, don't hold it against me. I only saw a very small part of the world of big business—my father's part—and I was silly enough to judge the whole of it by that one part. But I know better now. People are individuals, and you shouldn't make sweeping judgements.'

She smiled up at him under long lashes. 'I shall be very old-fashioned wife. Wherever you are and whatever you do will be OK with me, and I'm sure I shall like your friends. I'll do my best to preside over all the dinner-parties you care to arrange in the course of business. Who knows, I might even begin to understand the money market myself!' She sobered. 'I hope I've grown up quite a bit in the last few weeks, darling. When I think of the awful things I said to you it makes my blood run cold.'

Guy reached over and covered her hand with his. 'When I think that I let you go when I could have explained, if it hadn't been for my stiff-necked pride, it makes *my* blood run cold. I knew I forced you to marry me under duress, it was the only way I could think of to get you. I knew you didn't like me, you made no secret of that. So I set myself to make you fall in love with me and on our honeymoon I thought I'd succeeded. When I seemed to have failed it was the end of the world.'

She took his hand in hers and held it tightly and the warmth of it penetrated right through her body. 'We'll put it all behind us from now on,' she said. 'Agreed?'

'Agreed,' he said fervently, raising her hand and kissing each finger in turn.

Then he felt in his pocket and brought out an envelope. 'As we're dispelling old ghosts we may as well deal with this one too.'

Lucie took the envelope. 'It's from Peter.'

'I had an idea it might be. It was delivered to your father's villa—it must have come a few days ago. And if he's got any bright ideas about hanging around you again, he can forget them,' he added darkly.

Lucie tore open the envelope and read the short letter inside.

'My dearest Lucie,' Peter had written, 'I couldn't just let it go without telling you how absolutely chuffed I am. I'm actually in the process of starting up my own agency—and I positively insist on handling all your work in future. I promise to make you famous, with lots of lovely lolly, and it's the least I can do in view of the generosity of your papa. Of course I knew that he was paying me off to remove myself from the scene and leave the field clear for Devereux, but I reckoned you wouldn't be heart-broken about my departure. I think I knew all along that you were never in love with me and only agreed to our "engagement" to have a back-up on the trip. I hope by now you and Devereux will have fixed something up. The address of the agency is as above—you must come and see me in all my glory very soon. Yours as ever, Peter.'

Lucie handed the letter to Guy. 'He doesn't know—about Father. He left before it happened.'

Guy read the letter through and shook his head. They were both silent for a time, deep in their own thoughts.

Then Lucie said slowly, 'Guy, you know what this means, don't you? If Father paid Peter off to break his engagement to me it means that he must have had some last hope that you and I would get together and that you would use your influence in the bank to get him out of trouble. He *didn't* mean to die when he went on that dive. He meant to stay and fight.'

Guy nodded, his lips pursed. 'I worked that out for myself yesterday. I found your father's cheque-book with a largish sum paid out to Peter Philips. I didn't have to be Sherlock Holmes to solve that problem.'

Lucie put a hand over her eyes to hide the tears that welled up. 'I'm glad he didn't die in that terrible way. But—but it hurts that he *didn't* send for me because he loved me and wanted to make up our quarrel. I was still only a pawn in his game of high finance.' She choked over the words. 'And I was so glad we'd come together again and that he really cared about me. All he ever cared about was power and money.'

Guy came round the table and wrapped his arm round her. 'I doubt if people do change very much. But all the same I'm sure he *was* glad to see you, to feel you still cared about him. He must have been a very lonely man.'

Lucie looked up into the dark-lashed eyes that met her own with such understanding, and was overwhelmed by a rush of love and gratitude. She pressed her face against his chest as he stood behind her chair and knew with absolute certainty that the bad times were over and the future lay ahead, full of promise. 'Oh, Guy darling, I do love you so much,' she whispered unsteadily.

He slipped into a chair very close beside her, and said thoughtfully, 'I think I'll arrange to have an extra week off work—they can get along without me. How does the idea of a second honeymoon appeal to you?'

'Oh *yes*—wonderful! Where?' Lucie held her breath, willing him to take her back to "their" island. Not that she wouldn't have followed him gladly to any place in the world that he suggested,

but somehow that primitive little shack with none of
the creature comforts of high living seemed to
underline for her that there were many more sides to
Guy than she had once believed so mistakenly.

'Where?' The blue eyes twinkled into hers. 'Surely
there can only be one place?'

'The shack? Our very own honeymoon island?'

'Correct,' he said. 'We'll go over from the Brac by
sea and take lots of tins to replenish Derek's store,
and quite a few goodies for ourselves, too. We'll call
it our *second* honeymoon island, and I promise you it
will be an even better honeymoon than the first.'

'Couldn't be,' Lucie shook her head.

'Indeed it could. For now we know we love each
other, and then we loved each other without each
other knowing that we loved each other. Work that
one out, sweetheart.'

He put out a hand and pulled her lazily on to his
knees, and she twined her arms round his neck and
laid her face against his.

'I'm no good at puzzles,' she whispered. 'You can
show me what you mean when we get to our island.'

'I will, my dearest heart,' he promised, his mouth
against her soft cheek. 'Oh, I certainly will!'

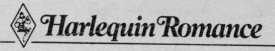**Harlequin Romance**

Coming Next Month

Available in January wherever paperback books are sold, or
through Harlequin Reader Service.

In the U.S.
901 Fuhrmann Blvd.
P.O. Box 1397
Buffalo, N.Y. 14240-1397

In Canada
P.O. Box 603
Fort Erie, Ontario
L2A 5X3

Harlequin Intrigue

In October
Watch for the new look of

Harlequin Intrigue
...because romance can be quite an adventure!

Each time, Harlequin Intrigue brings you great stories, mixing a contemporary, sophisticated romance with the surprising twists and turns of a puzzler...romance with "something more."

Plus...
in next month's publications of Harlequin Intrigue we offer you the chance to win one of four mysterious and exciting weekends. Don't miss the opportunity! Read the October Harlequin Intrigues!

ATTRACTIVE, SPACE SAVING BOOK RACK

Display your most prized novels on this handsome and sturdy book rack. The hand-rubbed walnut finish will blend into your library decor with quiet elegance, providing a practical organizer for your favorite hard-or soft-covered books.

Only $9.95

Approximately 16" x 8" when assembled

Assembles in seconds

To order, rush your name, address and zip code, along with a check or money order for $10.70* ($9.95 plus 75¢ postage and handling) payable to *Harlequin Reader Service*:

Harlequin Reader Service
Book Rack Offer
901 Fuhrmann Blvd.
P.O. Box 1396
Buffalo, NY 14269-1396

Offer not available in Canada.

*New York and Iowa residents add appropriate sales tax.